AYDIN

TN SEAL SECURITY BOOK 1

CHIQUITA DENNIE

304 PUBLISHING COMPANY

This book is dedicated to the readers that have been with me since day one. The support means a lot and you've helped me to follow my dreams.

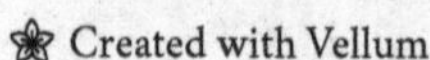 Created with Vellum

LATEST RELEASES

Latest Releases from Chiquita Dennie

The Early Years-A Prequel Short Story
Antonio and Sabrina: Struck in Love 1, 2, 3,4, 5
Heart of Stone, Book 1 (Emery & Jackson)
Heart Of Stone Book 1.5 Emery &Jackson A Valentine's Day Short
Janice and Carlo: Captivated By His Love
Heart of Stone, Book 2 (Jordan and Damon)
Temptation
Heart of Stone, Book 3 (Angela and Brent)
Cocky Catcher
Bossy Billionaire
Bottoms Up Heart of Stone, Book 3.5 (Jessica and Joseph Short
Love Shorts: A Collection of Short Stories
Joaquin Fuertes (The Fuertes Cartel Book 1)
Exposed (Salvation Society Novel)
Joaquin Fuertes (The Fuertes Cartel Book 2)
Refuel (A Driven World Novel)

Pressure (A Driven World Novel)
Until Serena (HEA World Novel)
Antonio and Sabrina: Struck in Love 5
Heart of Stone, Book 4 (Jessica and Joseph)
She's All I Need
Red Light District (A Fantasy Romance Short)
Something Gained (A Romantic Comedy Book1)
Aydin (TN Security Book 1)
Upcoming Releases (2022/2023):
Satin Hill (Book 1)
Dare To Love
Unveiled (Achille Cartel Book 1)
The Carrington Cartel Book 1

DISCLAIMER

This work of fiction contains strong language and explicit sexual content and is only intended for mature readers. This story may contain unconventional situations, language, and sexual encounters that may offend some readers. This book is for mature readers (18+).

INTRODUCTION

Are you signed up for my newsletter?

Join today and find out all the latest in new releases, contests, giveaways, sneak peeks and more.

www.chiquitadennie.com

AUTHOR NOTE:

I love suspenseful and romantic elements in my stories and that started with my mafia series. I decided to branch into military romance, romantic suspense after I wrote a few projects under other publishers. TN Security is a fictional world and based on my hometown of Memphis, Tennessee. You might notice a few real-life places described in this book. All books are standalone and inter-connected. Trigger Warning: kidnapping, torture, killing, and explicit content.

SYNOPSIS

Aydin is a strong, brave man. As a former Navy Seal, he's fought many battles with no fear... until he meets Amelia. She does something to him that he can't explain. The man known as the "Beast" by his colleagues isn't afraid of love. Or is he?

Amelia thinks she can handle her own, but when she's robbed on the street, she's powerless. Thankfully, a Good Samaritan arrives in the form of handsome Aydin.

The following day, she walks into a security firm looking for a new job. What she finds is her hero. Soon, they're swept up in an even more dangerous situation.

Can she trust Aydin with her life or is the risk too much to take?

Aydin is the first standalone book in an interconnected TN Seal Security series. If you're looking for a grumpy-boss, workplace, Suspenseful steamy romance, you'll love Aydin.

"Damn it!" I blurted out, rubbing the scrape on my exposed thigh. After I finished my last interview a few hours ago, I ventured out for a drink to wind down. I felt my phone vibrate, and I snapped it out of my pocket to see my mom texting me.

"She's probably worried," I muttered to myself, keying in my code to unlock the screen and accessing my messages while I walked down the street.

Mom: *How did it turn out?*

Me: *I think I got this one.*

"Don't scream, or I'll cut your throat," a gravelly voice commanded.

Initially shocked, I froze and scanned around the street for help, but it was late at night, and most people's attention was on themselves.

"Give me your money!" He pointed a knife at me as he stood before me wearing a skull mask and black gloves.

"I don't have any," I stuttered, praying someone caught on to what was going on.

"Stop lying!" he hissed, jerking the knife at my face. So I

removed the strap from my shoulder and handed over my purse. As I reached into my jacket pocket, the keys fell out. The man rummaged through my wallet and cursed under his breath. With each step, I moved away from him, confident that he wouldn't find anything inside other than my ID and maybe five dollars. As soon as he noticed her, he threw it to the ground.

"Bitch! Come here." He charged at me.

"I'm sorry!" I staggered backwards.

"Hey, move the fuck away from her!" A growl followed by a large hand pushing me to the side stopped me in my tracks. The moment I saw him pick him up by the throat, I covered my eyes.

"She's... lying," the guy pleaded.

My savior was tall, had a buzz cut, and towered over the man who tried to rob me.

"You like picking on someone. Try that shit with me."

"Nuke!" I heard another deep voice yell, and the large man in front of me dropped the robber on the ground.

"He's not worth it. Get out of here." The new guy, wearing the leather jacket, told the robber.

"Thank you," I said, and they turned around. I felt my breath catch in my throat as thoughts of the sexy savior filled my mind.

"Did he touch you?" He lifted my chin to examine my face.

"No, just a little shook up," I responded nervously and wiped my hands down my jacket.

"I'm Nasir, and this is Aydin." Another tall, buff gentleman introduced himself. He was just as mesmerizing.

"Amelia," I replied and shook his hand.

"Where's your car?" Aydin probed.

I motioned my hand to the yellow Volkswagen parked at the corner.

"We can walk you to your car."

"Uh… thanks."

"What are you doing out here by yourself?" Nasir asked.

All three of us headed toward my car. Aydin stood at the driver's side, and when I popped the key in, he pulled the door open.

"Thanks. I had an interview in the area."

"Yeah, this area can get pretty rough if you're not paying attention," Nasir responded, but Aydin glared at me like I'd said something wrong.

"Surprisingly, this was the first time I've been held at knife point." I shut the door and slid the key in the ignition.

"Try to pay attention next time," Aydin quipped, and I felt like a little girl getting chastised.

"I mean I didn't expect to have a deranged man at my throat when I came out of a bar."

We had a stare off for a few minutes.

"Yo, Aydin! Nasir!" A loud voice called their names and broke her stare off.

"Nicco is probably cheating. We need to get back," Nasir announced, and I put the turn signal on and watched them head back to the bar I'd just come out of. I passed the three of them standing in front talking and shook my head at what almost happened.

Thirty minutes later, I arrived home and took the elevator to my place on the second floor. The apartment I might lose if none of the interviews I went to call me back. After removing my jacket and kicking off my heels, I went to the kitchen and saw my leftover ravioli was still in the fridge. Often, my best friend would come over and eat me out of house and home even though she lived just upstairs. I removed the plastic and placed the food in the microwave, set to the highest temperature. At thirty-five, I shouldn't be in this predicament. I'd always prided myself on being responsible. But the past year had shown me even the best intentions weren't always the safest. Being that my ex up and left me to marry his ex and stuck me with all the bills, I had to come to terms with Bradley not putting forth an effort the way I thought he did. I wasn't naive, but when I loved, I loved hard. All my life, it'd been that way. I had my parents to thank for showing me that a real marriage was possible. They'd been together for over thirty years, raised me in a three-bedroom home with my two sisters, put me through college, and taught me to love myself. But the men I'd come across seemed to take me for a fool. The bell on the microwave chimed and after grabbing the fork to eat at the table, I noticed the red light on my voicemail blinking. Dismissing the food for a second, I angled over to the wall that held the cordless phone and hit play.

"Hello, Amelia, this is Molly from TN Security. We'd love to have you come aboard. Please come tomorrow to fill out your paperwork."

"I got the job," I muttered to myself, checked my watch, and saw it was going on ten at night.

"Shit! I need to find the best outfit for tomorrow." I grabbed my food and ran out of the kitchen to my bedroom to rummage my closet.

"Office attire. I need something sharp." I picked through the rack of pantsuits I'd compiled over the years and decided to go with a black jumpsuit with a high waist and belt attached.

I laid the outfit on the chair in my bedroom and bent down to grab a pair of my favorite high-heeled shoes. TN Security was the last place I interviewed with after a long week of not hearing anything back. I lost my job a month ago because my car broke down, and my boss was an asshole who somehow thought the world revolved around him. During this time, I was still dealing with the breakup, and everything that could go wrong went wrong from a bad pregnancy scare, cheating boyfriend, my bank account getting withdrawn to zero, then a car breakdown. Now, starting over fresh, I needed to figure out my next moves if I wanted to show my sisters that I didn't need to rely on them for help. I pinned my hair up into a bun, threw on my scarf to protect my braids, and headed to the bathroom to shower and brush my teeth.

Ring!

"Ughhh, who could that be?" I marched back into the living room to remove my cell from my purse and saw Dani's name scroll across.

"Hello," I answered, dropping my purse on the couch and checking to make sure I locked the door, and went back to my bedroom.

"How did the interviews go?"

"Terrible," I slid the shower curtain back, turned the knob, and checked to make sure I had the right temperature.

"You can always come work with me."

Dani worked as a bottle girl at a local bar, and I refused to work for that sleazeball of a boss she had. The money was good, but I'd have to be subjected to a host of egomaniacs who thought they could talk to me in any kind of way.

"I appreciate the offer, but I got a call back tonight."

"Really, where?"

I placed the call on speaker, put it down on the counter, and removed my clothes.

"Secretary job at a security firm."

"Oh, well, that sounds nice."

"Yeah, it's the only place that called back."

"You have to stay positive, Amelia."

"You're right. Until I can replenish my savings account, I have to do what I can."

"Have you heard from him?"

"No, and I hope I never hear from him again."

"He's a sorry excuse of a man."

"Tell me about it, but I need to jump in the shower and head to bed. First day is tomorrow."

"Wow! That's fast."

"They'll probably give me a tour and fill out paperwork."

"That's true."

"Talk tomorrow."

"So no breakfast in the morning?"

I shook my head in the mirror. Depending on our schedules, one of us would get up and cook breakfast if we had the time and invite the other person over.

"Not this time, crazy lady."

She chuckled.

"All right, call me on your lunch break tomorrow."

"Will do. Good night."

"Night."

* * *

THE NEXT MORNING.

I slammed my hand down on the alarm to turn it off and rubbed a hand down my face. Thirty minutes later, after showering and getting dressed, I parked in the visitors section and went to the front door, rubbing my stomach to calm my nerves.

"You can do this," I mumbled to myself, opened the front door of TN Security, smiled, and walked up to the reception desk.

"Hi, give me a minute," the girl at the front desk requested. She looked overwhelmed with the amount of calls constantly going off. I stood at the corner of the desk, while people came and went through the office. The place was a ten-story building in downtown Memphis, adjacent to my favorite barbeque spot.

"Sorry about that, how can I help you?"

"Hi, I was left a voice message yesterday about the secretary position."

"What's your name?"

She started to type on her computer.

"Amelia Edwards."

"Oh, yes, that was me. I'm Molly, the front receptionist."

"Hi, nice to meet you."

"So, I know you applied for the secretary position, but it's been taken."

"Huh… that fast?"

"Yeah. I need to hurry up and get things moving. Your new position is Operations manager and assistant to the owner."

"Wait, Operations manager?" I dropped my hands to my side.

"I know, but your resume shows you have experience, and you went to school for accounting."

"Well…"

"Molly, did my lunch come in yet?" I heard a familiar voice and when I looked up, it was the guy named Nasir from last night.

"Nasir, I'm not your secretary. Order your own food," Molly fussed and waved him off.

"Do I know you from somewhere?" he asked.

"She's the new Operations manager and Aydin's assistant."

My head whipped around at her statement.

"Wait, I think you have me mixed up."

"Ohh, well, good luck with that."

"Don't listen to him. Aydin is harmless."

Nasir laughed and walked off.

"He's an ass. So, are you going to take the job?" Molly held out a clipboard with paperwork to fill out.

"Yeahhh… Yes, I'll take the job." I didn't have any choice at this point. My rent was due next month, and begging my parents or sister wasn't an option.

"Great. Take these forms, and I'll show you to your office."

"An office?"

Molly came around the desk and pointed toward the elevator. I trailed behind and listened to her explain the duties.

"You'll basically keep Aydin focused and on track. He's the owner of TN Security."

"Wouldn't that make you the Operations manager?"

She waved me off.

"Nope, I have enough responsibility. Besides, I'm getting married in a month and plan to take some time off."

"Who's going to run the front desk?"

"That's why I hired temporary staff."

Ding!

We stepped off on the tenth floor, and I followed her down the hall to a wooden door. She pushed the key inside, and it automatically unlocked. My mouth dropped in shock. The place was the size of two offices; even my living room wasn't this big. It had cream carpeting, large, plush pillows on the couch, wide, long windows, a glass table, and artwork that I couldn't take my eyes off.

"What do you think?"

"Are you sure this is my office?"

She chuckled.

"Yes, it's your office." Molly took my coat out of my hand.

"Are you positive they said they would hire me for this position?"

"Your experience speaks for itself. Fill out everything, and we'll get you the keys to the office."

"Okay, I forgot to ask. How much does the position pay?"

"Seventy thousand a year, plus benefits."

"Wow."

"Before I head to lunch, I want to introduce you to who you'll report to."

"The owner, right?"

"Yes. I have to warn you, he can be a little grumpy with new people, but he's a sweetheart after you get to know him."

"Maybe I should have met him before you showed me the office." I chuckled, and she laughed, waving me off.

"He trusts my judgment, so you're a good choice in my book," she commented. I put the paperwork down on the desk and walked alongside her to his office. The building wasn't decorated to be an inviting space. It felt more like a doctor's office, cold with no pictures on the wall, and the furniture was mostly black leather couches. Molly tapped on the door lightly before pushing it open. I heard a low growl like an animal, and my head popped up and saw it was the same guy from last night who helped me during the mugging.

"Aydin, are you busy?" Molly probed, strolled toward him, and picked up some folders from his desk. He stared back at me, and I felt a lump in my throat at seeing him during the daylight. I knew he was handsome, but he had more of a mystery to him. His striking gray eyes looked back at me. The intensity in his jawline as he gritted his teeth looked like he was ready to scold me for doing something wrong.

"Always busy," he fussed and turned his eyes away to face Molly.

"Well, this is Amelia, and she's going to be the new Operations manager," Molly informed him, and his eyebrows rose in surprise.

"When was this decided?" he questioned.

"You said, and I quote, *Molly, handle it.*"

"I can go…" I muttered, not wanting to cause a problem. At the same time, I needed a job.

"You're hired, Amelia. He's just having a bad day," Molly fussed, planting her hands on her hip

"Molly."

"I'm not listening. She's qualified and ready to start."

"Fine. You train her, and I mean the minute she fucks up, it's on you." He pointed a finger at her, then Molly flipped him off. I'd never seen an employee act this way with their boss.

"Ignore him, Amelia. You'll do fine."

"Thanks."

"I have a meeting in thirty minutes. Can you get her up to speed, or do I need to do that?" Aydin asked.

"No worries, she'll be ready with bells on, Mr. Grumpy Pants," Molly teased, turned toward me, and interlocked our arms. Walking out of his office, I felt the butterflies leave my stomach. Molly escorted me to the breakroom, supply office, and bathrooms along with a few employees.

"Here's your office again." Molly unlocked the door. I went around to my desk and sat, situating myself and checking out the drawers and computer.

"I have lunch, so you'll have to sit in on the meeting by yourself," Molly said.

"Okay, anything I should know?"

"Nothing major. Mostly, they run through what clients they have for the week."

"Actually, I know Aydin."

"Really! From where?"

"He saved me from a mugger last night."

"Oh, see that shows you it's meant for you to have this position."

"Hopefully, it won't be awkward."

"No, you'll be fine."

"Thanks, Molly."

"You're welcome. Here's the information on TN Security. Study what you can, but the meeting starts in thirty minutes."

"I'll do that now."

"Great, see you when I get back."

"Have a great lunch."

Molly bowed like I was a king on a throne, walked out of the office, and left me to get familiar with the day-to-day business.

AYDIN

Out of all the places for me to run into the woman I couldn't keep my mind off all last night in my dreams, she walked right through my door. Something told me it would be a problem, and I needed to fire her immediately before I crossed that line. Already I wanted to protect her from anything or anyone who tried to cause her any pain. The way her round, doe eyes looked back at me caused my dick to jump in my pants. I tried to control my attitude, but it was hard as Molly was talking about her being the Operations manager and my assistant. It probably looked bad that I gritted my teeth and almost squeezed the life out of my stress ball. Before Amelia stepped into my office, another crisis had come up with one of my clients, and they needed to hire my team to handle security for an overseas trip. We'd been booked up for the past few months. I opened TN Security a few years back after I left the navy and brought along the people who worked with me every day. Nasir and Rocco were just a few of my guys. When I decided to start this business, I needed loyal people around me who would carry on my values even if I wasn't there.

Knock! Knock!

The door opened, and Nasir stepped inside with an annoyed expression on his face. I had an idea of what he was about to talk about, and I felt the same way.

"I read over the email and was already stretched thin," Nasir stated, as he sat in the chair and ran a hand down his face.

"Clarence just called to see if I changed my mind."

"He knows how to annoy me, because he texted me yesterday," Nasir informed me. Clarence, our longtime client, expected us to drop everything to accommodate his family.

"We're booked up, and I told him that already."

"Are you ready for the meeting?"

"Yeah."

"What's wrong with you?"

"Molly hired a new Operations manager."

"So?"

"It's the woman from last night."

"What!"

I nodded and stood out of my seat.

"Just as surprised as you when she stepped in my office."

"Is she qualified? What's her name?"

"Amelia."

"Amelia," he repeated. My stomach tightened at his mention of her name. I had no claim on her, but to hear another guy call her name did something to me.

"Why are you looking like that?"

"Like what?" I replied.

"Like you're ready to kick my ass for saying her name."

Nasir chuckled, and I flipped him off and followed him out of the office.

"Time for the meeting."

"Are you leading this meeting?" Nasir questioned, and I shook my head. His lips formed into a thin line. He always led the meetings and today, he thought it would be different because of a new employee.

"You're the owner, but you refuse to lead meetings."

"Why do I have you as my second in charge?"

He laughed, and we walked toward the conference room, and most of our staff were in attendance. Nasir opened the door, and I went to my usual seat in the back, so I could watch everyone's expression when certain details were explained. Amelia sat next to Carly, one of our tech assistants, near the front, and I watched Nasir extend his hand out to Amelia. Then he pointed at me. That gesture caused Amelia to look over her shoulder at me. Nicco came in last as usual and took a seat next to me. He wore shades, since last night he got pretty wasted.

"Before we get started, let's welcome Amelia to the team," Nasir announced. Everyone in the room clapped. Amelia seemed embarrassed to be the center of attention but thanked Nasir and Molly.

"Can we get started?" I huffed, clasping my hands together and sat forward in the chair.

"Amelia, he might be your boss, but we all ignore him," Nasir joked.

She smiled and opened the notebook in front of her to take notes.

"We have two events this week. Nicco is leading the extraction team Adonis," Nasir informed the group. Nicco nodded and sat back in his chair.

"The next mission is the senator's daughter," I said. Everyone glanced back at me.

Senator Edgar's daughter, Addison, was visiting Chicago for a few days, and she requested for our team to accompany her.

"I thought Addison decided not to run for election again?" Nicco wondered, and I did tell them that a few weeks ago. Addison was more ambitious than her father, and many times she'd been in the news for doing something to get further ahead for the upcoming election cycle.

"It's one event she needs us to provide security and potential fundraisers."

"Do you need Carly to get background checks started?"

"If she can have it done by the end of the week, make it a priority."

"Amelia can help," Nasir suggested. Amelia gasped in surprise.

"Uhmm... Do you think it's too soon?" Amelia questioned.

"You'll be fine. It won't take long with Carly helping," Nasir answered.

"Anything else?" I looked around the room at my team.

"Nicco, get your team rounded up, and Aydin, let me know how many guys you need," Nasir said.

"How are things looking overall?" Nicco asked.

"Aydin, do you want to talk about it, or should I?" Nasir questioned.

"TN Security handles high-profile cases and a few celebrities, but we've recently seen an increase in our services being used for political cases."

"That's good, right?" Carly asked.

"Maybe, but it depends on the clients."

"Wait, are you talking about enemies of the US?" Amelia blurted out.

"Something like that."

"How do you determine who to work with?" Amelia

asked. Nasir glanced from her to me, waiting for an answer.

"That's why we're meeting now. Yes, we vet our clients, but sometimes things fall through the crack."

"What Aydin is trying to say is that we need to be on high alert at all times," Nasir explained. Everyone nodded in agreement.

"I have a few calls to make, and then I'm leaving for the day." I stood from the chair and headed toward the door.

"Excuse me, Mr. Reeve." Amelia jumped up from her seat, and all eyes watched her run after me.

"Call me Aydin."

"Uhmm, Aydin. Should we meet to talk about your schedule?" Amelia looked up at me. I felt like shit, because being in her presence for too long, and the perfume that lingered in the air, caused a reaction I didn't want to surface.

"Molly knows what I need."

I started to walk away, but she grasped my arm. I looked down, and she released me.

"Sorry, but Molly wanted me to check with you to get a firsthand account."

"For now, check over emails, messages, and inventory orders." I didn't have time to babysit anyone, and Molly would hear about this when she got back.

"Okay, should I order your lunch, or will you handle that?"

My back was turned to her, and I smirked at her little feisty attitude. I wanted to teach her a lesson without my employees finding out.

I grunted. "I'll handle that." Continuing toward my office, my cell phone rang. I slipped it out of my pocket and saw Addison's name pop up. Deciding to call her back after I was done with other clients, I let the call go to voicemail.

* * *

LATER IN THE AFTERNOON, I finished lunch with Nasir and Nicco, then decided to finish off the work day at home. After grabbing my keys, cell phone, and jacket to leave the office, I locked up my computer and headed to Amelia's office to let her know.

I tapped on her door and waited for her to answer.

"Mr. Reeve," she answered, stood at the door, and looked from behind her. I saw Molly sitting in the chair with food scattered about.

"I'm about to leave for the day."

"Ohhh…" She sounded disappointed in the statement.

"Molly can help you with any other questions."

Amelia looked back at Molly.

"Aydin's not this grumpy all the time, Amelia," Molly confessed, and I rolled my eyes at her statement.

"Thanks, Molly." I slid my hands in my pockets.

"Well, I'd like to go over the budget with you sometime this week," Amelia suggested, and I agreed.

"Tomorrow, I can set time to discuss the budget." I lifted my watch to check the time.

"Thank you."

"And call me Aydin."

"Right, Aydin. Sorry, Mr. Reev… I mean Aydin," she stuttered. Molly burst into laughter.

"Anyway, I'll be on call if you have an emergency."

"Sure. See you tomorrow." Amelia and I stood for a moment before she cleared her throat and closed the door.

"Snap out of it," I mumbled to myself and headed out of

the office for the day. At my Ford truck, I hopped inside and released a breath.

"No dating rule."

A policy was enforced right at the very start of TN Security to not date co-workers because it always ended badly and messed up business for everyone. Nasir thought I was crazy to try to tell adults what to do, but it was my business at the end of the day, and I'd like to avoid getting sued. I pulled out of the parking lot, turned into traffic, and headed to my parents' house to check in since I'd missed a few dinners lately. As the oldest of three boys, I'd prided myself on setting an example for my brothers, and commitment to family was our biggest thing. After I served in the navy, I was away for years and only saw them through video calls or visits when I got approved time away. Overall, my parents were excited when I told them I'd be home for good and would open my own business with consistent hours that I could set for myself. I didn't have a wife and wasn't even in the process of wanting one. Women in general couldn't handle my lifestyle in the security business. Sometimes we had long hours or had to leave the country in less than twenty-four-hours' notice. I arrived at my parents' home a few miles from my place and parked in the driveway. We didn't grow up rich. Everything we had was from my parents' work ethic and instilling in us that if we wanted something, we had to go out and get a job to have it rather than ask for a handout. As I walked up to the door, it came open and saw the family dog run toward me.

"Nuke, get down!" Mom yelled. The dog was a golden retriever, and they named him after my nickname in the navy, Aydin "Nuke" Reeve. It was a shock when I got home from my second tour, and he jumped all over me like he was doing now, and we completely spoiled him.

"Good boy, Nuke." I ran a hand across his head and patted his cheek.

I whistled, and he followed me inside the house.

"He's getting big," I said, leaning down to hug my mom.

"Because your father doesn't know how to say no," Mom hissed and shut the door behind me. She nudged Nuke to sit down, and he followed me to the kitchen instead. That was another drawback; they complained even though he was their dog, Nuke only listened to me most of the time.

"How was work today?" Mom probed, and I opened the fridge to grab a beer and stood next to the table to watch her prepare a salad.

"Busy."

She stopped pouring the pasta in the draining bowl and turned toward me. Rebecca Reeve was tougher than Dad, and I could never get away with anything. Dad was soft toward us. We could stay up late on school nights or go to parties, but Mom would be the one to discipline us if we got out of hand.

"Did you finally hire someone?"

"Someone." I picked up a piece of cucumber she cut up and tossed it in my mouth.

Mom glanced up at me.

"What does that mean?"

"Mom!" Wesley's loud voice echoed through the house.

Wesley stepped in the kitchen holding a bag of groceries and dropped them on the table.

"If you were here early, you should have picked this stuff up," Wesley argued, and I grinned. Mom would often make one of us grab last-minute items from the store if we got to the house first. Wesley looked annoyed, and I wanted to laugh, but that would cause Wesley to try to fight me.

"Sorry, little bro. You had it today."

"Shut up," Wesley mumbled, and Mom popped him on the hand with a wooden spoon.

"Don't be rude, Wesley."

He rubbed the sore hand, as Mom turned back around, and he flipped me off. I burst into laughter.

"What are you cooking for dinner?" Wesley asked, leaning over her shoulder. Dad was about six-one, short, brown hair, and was still muscular in shape in his late fifties, while Mom was the shortest in the family. She was about five-five, small but feisty, and I took my temper from her, along with the protectiveness from my father.

"Wash your hands. Dinner will be ready soon," Mom told us.

I went to sit next to my brother, removed my cell from my pocket, and laid it on the table, when the door opened and closed again.

"Aydin, you parked in my spot!" Josiah, the youngest of the group, yelled.

"Josiah, stop that yelling," Mom fussed, wiping her hands. Josiah leaned over to kiss her cheek and popped Wesley on the back of the head. I shook hands with him before he opened the fridge and grabbed a beer to sit across from me.

"Where's Dad?" Josiah questioned. Dad came in the kitchen and groped Mom from behind and kissed her cheek.

"Ugh, can you two do that somewhere else?" Wesley hissed.

"Shut up!" Mom shouted, and we all laughed at her response.

"Josiah, did you pull your car up?" Cole Reeve lifted the plate of stuffed peppers from the stove and placed them on the table.

Josiah scooped some of the salad and peppers, then filled his glass with beer.

"Even though Aydin stole my spot," Josiah teased. I chuckled, scanning my eyes down at my phone as Addison's name ran across. I ignored the call and focused on my food when it rang again.

"Who is calling you back-to-back?" Wesley inquired, smearing dressing over his salad.

"A client."

"Must be important for them to call back-to-back."

"They can wait."

"Did you tell them about me working at the security firm?" Josiah brought up.

Josiah was twenty-five and just graduated from college. He was good with technology, so for a way to get him in the working field, I decided to hire him to oversee our department. Wesley was thirty and acted like a teenager most times we were together, but he was smart and worked as a cop.

"That's wonderful, Josiah," Mom said, patting his palm. She extended more food to us all as we continued talking about Josiah working with me at the office.

"You'll start tomorrow."

"Great. I have an idea to set up a new security system."

"Just make sure you don't end up on the FBI list."

"Can't promise you that, bro," Josiah joked.

I shook my head and finished the rest of my food. For the next two hours, we laughed and watched movies together. I finally made it home and showered right after to fall into bed and prepare for the week with Addison's attitude.

*R*ing! I slammed my hand down on the alarm clock and rolled over, rubbing my eyes. It was going on my third day at the job, and I was still trying to cope with the workload. Molly had been a big help, but most of the time, Aydin had been in and out of the office, avoiding me for what reasons I had no clue. Today, I made a promise to myself to get a few moments of his time to run through some of the accounts they handled.

"Lia!" I heard the loud, boisterous voice of my best friend, Dani, come into my place.

We had keys to each other's apartment for emergencies, but she didn't care what day or time, she'd just show up without knocking.

"There you are." Dani pushed my bedroom door open as I sat up in my bed.

"Why are you here so early?" I looked at the time on my alarm clock. It was eight fifteen, and I needed to be at work nine thirty.

"I brought breakfast." Dani held a cup of coffee out for

me, dropped the bag of food on the bed, and sat in the chair in the corner of my room. Before I lost my job, I'd redecorated and added a TV on the wall and a bookcase next to the chair for the nights I wanted to chill with a glass of wine and read.

"Shouldn't you be at work?" I sipped on the coffee and reached in the bag to pull out a cinnamon raisin bagel.

"I have a little bit of time."

I opened the cream cheese, spread it across, and took a bite.

"This is good and warm."

"See? I knew you needed that."

"Only reason you brought breakfast is because you want something."

Her eyes crinkled in confusion.

"Don't lie." I pointed at her.

"Fine, I have a date this weekend."

"Nope."

"You haven't even heard the question."

I slid the covers back, rose out of bed, and headed to get ready for the day.

"Amelia, you need to have fun."

"You have enough fun for both of us." I pinned my hair up and sauntered to the shower, setting it to the hottest temperature.

"A nice dinner with a friend, nothing more," Dani explained. If anything, she wanted me to give an opinion of her date and feel him out. The friend was probably one who wanted a one-night stand, and that wasn't my style, but I talked about women who could have sex without knowing the person.

"Sorry, Dani, I have too much work." She groaned and complained about me staying in the house all the time, and I chuckled at her groveling. Fifteen minutes later, I stepped out of the shower and went to my closet to pick out a nice pantsuit for today.

"That's what you're wearing?" Dani questioned, her face scrunched up at my blue-stripe suit.

"Yeah. It's cute."

"You're an office manager; that outfit makes you look boring."

"This is fine."

We'd gotten dressed in front of each other over the years, so it was natural for us to see each other naked. I ran a hand down the white blouse I tucked in my pants and picked up the short jacket to button.

"Pair the red shoes to give you a little sparkle."

"That's a good idea." I bent down to find the red Marc Jacobs heels I purchased a few years back.

"So how is the job going?"

"Well, my boss is a little distant, but everyone else is fine."

"What do you mean distant?"

"Not sure, he just seems like I'm bothering him."

"This is the security company, right?" she stated, flipping through a magazine. I laid on a little lip gloss and eyeshadow, released my hair to hang down, placed my glasses on, and turned around.

"Yes, how do I look?"

"Cute. But is the boss rude to you?"

"No, just always busy."

"Interesting."

"Very, but let's go so I'm not late."

"How are you doing with rent?"

"I talked to my landlord and explained I got a new job so I should be caught up soon."

She shut the door behind her and locked up.

"So, about this weekend..."

"Ughh, Dani, if this will shut you up. I'll go."

"Yayyy!" She reached over to hug me.

"Text me the time and place."

"I will, and don't let your boss walk all over you."

I slid into my car and shut the door, locking in my phone on the holder.

"Call me later!" she shouted and drove off as I turned the key in the ignition and reversed out of the driveway, heading to the office. My thoughts were all over the place with how I'd get Aydin to sit with me and talk over the details of how things were getting busy. Nasir had been great with checking in with me and invited me to lunch with the other people in the office.

Twenty minutes later, I arrived at work and parked in a reserved spot for employees.

"Morning! You look fabulous today," Molly said.

I waved to Molly as I entered the building. "Thanks, I feel good."

"How has the week been so far?"

She stood, came around the desk, and walked alongside me to my office. I turned the knob and draped my coat on the back of the door.

"The week has gone well. I still need to go through a few things with Aydin."

"He's in today."

"Great. Hopefully, he gives me a little of his time."

"You have to be a little pest with him."

I chuckled, shook my head, and checked over my messages.

"Is he in a good mood?"

"I mean it's Aydin; he's always in a mood." She laughed.

"Are you ready for time off?"

"Yes, finally I'm confident that you'll be able to handle things."

Ding!

A message came through on my email, and I clicked to read through the documents but noticed a few numbers looked off.

"Hummm…"

"What?"

"I don't know, maybe I'm overthinking."

"What are you talking about?"

"The event that Aydin is doing for the senator's daughter is a little weird."

"Addison's weird."

"How so?"

"She tries everything possible to get him to date her."

"I think I've seen her in pictures. She's pretty."

"She's annoying and uptight."

"Well, the amount of people she wants to cover the event doesn't match up with the costs."

"Tell Aydin."

"You're right."

"Anything else?" Molly stood behind the chair.

"No, for right now, just this issue with the senator."

"The event is this weekend; usually I go. You should attend."

"I don't think I should."

"Why not? Aydin and the guys will be there, and it brings in business."

"I'll think about it."

"Stop stressing. You've done a great job so far. Glad you came aboard."

"Thanks, Molly."

Molly waved me off and left my office. I continued reading all the emails and replying to new clients that wanted to hire the company. When I scanned the time, I saw it was going on eleven and decided to check in with

Aydin. I printed out the information on Addison's event and strolled down to his door and knocked.

"It's open."

I pushed the door open and smiled at him, but his face held no emotion.

"Morning."

"Morning."

"Is this a bad time?"

"No, what do you need?"

"I can come back."

"Obviously something is bothering you." He sat back in his chair.

"I received an email from Senator Edgar about the upcoming event with his daughter, and the numbers were off."

"By how much?" He leaned forward in his chair.

"My estimate is around five thousand."

"Send me the numbers." He looked up at me.

"Okay."

"Anything else?" He motioned his hand to continue.

I started to say something else but turned to leave, then froze and released a breath.

"Did I do something wrong?"

"Excuse me?"

"You seem frustrated with me, and I don't know why."

"I think you're overthinking."

"No, I'm not." My voice rose.

He tilted his head to the left.

"If you have something to say, spit it out."

"I didn't do anything to you, and you've ignored me since I started here."

"Are we in high school?"

"You know what, never mind," I hissed and turned to walk out of his office.

"Stop!" he shouted, and I froze.

I heard a low growl and felt the prickle of his breath on the back of my neck.

"I didn't hire you. So don't walk around here like you need my approval."

Something in me fired up in my gut, and I spun around. We were face-to-face with him towering over me. I might be quiet and nonchalant to avoid confrontation, but if anyone tried to make me seem like I was needy, then I'd be ready to curse them out.

"Listen, Mr. Reeve." I pointed a finger in his face.

"Aydin."

"Huh?"

"Call me Aydin."

"You're my boss. I'd rather keep it professional."

He stepped forward, and I felt a lump form in my throat.

"Aydin is what you're going to call me."

"But I—"

He cut me off.

"As I said, we're not in high school."

"Fine, but I need to know what you want to do about the renovation on the third floor."

"Handle it yourself. We have a budget."

"I understand, but the contractors you hired overestimated."

"Are you some whiz at numbers?"

"Something like that."

"Send me the breakdown."

"All right. Thanks, Mr.… I mean Aydin."

He cocked a left brow.

"Hey… Aydin. Am I interrupting something?" Nicco approached us and glanced from Aydin to me. Our eyes never left each other, and I couldn't understand why he was being so difficult toward me. I didn't beg for the job; I thought they would have hired someone more experienced.

"No, we're done," Aydin said, and I drew my eyes away and turned to leave. I shut the door to my office with my back against it and my eyes closed.

"Relax, he's your boss," I repeated over and over.

* * *

As FOOD WAS PLACED in front of us, I laughed at something Nasir said and avoided eye contact with Aydin, while he stared a hole in my face. As the new hire, Molly decided to treat me to lunch, and Nasir found out and invited himself, on top of paying, so everyone came along. We came to a local burger joint around the corner from the office. My plan was to originally eat at my desk and do more work.

"So, Amelia, where are you from?" Nasir challenged me. I washed the french fry down with myginger ale. Born and raised here in Tennessee, my parents spoiled me as the only child, and I never had to want for anything. Conrad and Cassandra Edwards had been married for over thirty years, and they had me in their late thirties. What I admired about my parents was how much their own individuality drew them together and not what the other person could do for them.

"Here in Tennessee."

"Any siblings?" Nasir wondered, and I shook my head.

"Only child."

"Lucky you. I grew up in a household of six," Molly complained, and I smiled.

"Well, I have my best friend, Dani, and she's like an annoying older sister." I chuckled, picking up my burger to take a bite.

"Did Aydin tell you about the event we're doing security for this weekend?"

"No."

"It's for Senator Edgar's daughter, and you're invited. We all get dressed up."

"What type of an event?" I drew a snarl from Aydin, and I wanted to poke his eye out for acting like a child. I knew what he was discussing, since Molly filled me in earlier.

"It's a fundraiser; she's thinking of running for office," Nasir answered, and I wiped the remnants of the ketchup from my face.

"I'm new; I doubt I should be there."

"We're all going to be there, you'll be fine. Well, we're doing security, so you can just mingle," Nasir said.

"Not sure if I have anything to wear."

"Every woman has a little cocktail dress," Molly brought up, and I scratched behind my ear and avoided eye contact with Aydin.

"What time is the fundraiser?"

"Eight, and you can drive with Aydin," Molly blurted out, and I choked on the drink as Aydin glared at her.

"No."

"Aydin, it's not like you're going to be taking a date," Molly stated, and Nasir chuckled, Aydin ran a hand down his face.

"I said no," Aydin responded, finishing off his sandwich, stood, and slid his hand in his pocket to remove his wallet to pay.

"What's his problem?" Molly quizzed. Nasir shrugged his shoulders.

"Beats me, but we can have a car pick you up, Amelia."

"You don't have to do that, Nasir. I can drive myself."

"Are you sure?"

"Yes, I don't plan on being there all night."

"If you change your mind, text me." Nasir followed in Aydin's steps and took money out to pay the bill.

"Ignore Aydin; the fundraiser is more than likely going to be boring."

"Molly, maybe I should find something else. Mr. Reeve seems to really hate me."

"He doesn't hate you. He's just an asshole."

"Okay, but please don't volunteer me for any other events."

She laughed, and we continued to discuss the fundraiser and her upcoming wedding plans.

Forty minutes later, I left work early, and Molly closed the office, so I decided to run by the nail shop to get a last-minute fill in before the weekend. Dani called, and I answered as I parked the car in front of the shop I frequent.

"Hello." I stepped out and closed the door, strolling to the front entrance.

"How was work?"

"It was good for the most part." I held my hand out to the receptionist, and she motioned for me to take the first seat at the front bar.

"The new boss?"

"Hard to tell."

"Hard to tell what?"

"He's one minute avoiding me and the next minute yelling at me."

"Wait, yelling about what?"

"Well not yelling exactly, but he's really big and grouchy."

"What!" She laughed through the phone.

"If you're going to laugh at me, I'm hanging up."

"I'm sorry, but that's hilarious."

"You find anything funny at my expense."

She cackled, and I chuckled under my breath.

"Where are you at?"

"At the nail salon."

"Ooh, someone's getting pretty for a date."

"It's not a date."

"You haven't gone out in months. Amelia, relax a little."

"For your information, I am relaxed. I plan on having a good time, but I'm not worried about your little setup."

"He's a cool guy."

"Again, I'm going to get free food and drink."

"Ugh, you're such a snob."

I giggled and changed hands for the technician to work on my left index finger.

"Where are we going?"

"A nice restaurant."

"I have another event this weekend. So, I can't stay out long."

"What event?"

"A work thing."

"Mmmmmm…"

"No, Dani."

"You don't know what I'm about to say."

"I can feel your vibe."

"You need a date for the event."

"I'm not taking anyone you know."

"Why? Are you trying to entice that boss of yours?" She giggled on the other end of the phone.

"Please, that man can't stand me."

"You need to get laid and forget about everything else."

"So I can turn into you?"

"Yes, a very happy woman with many orgasms."

We both laughed and continued to discuss what she was planning to wear, and I mentioned the dress I had from last Christmas that was still new and untouched. By the time I got home, it was going on eight at night, so I relaxed with takeout and watched movies for the rest of the night. Saturday was the double date, then on Sunday, the charity event would introduce me to a new world. I wasn't sure I'd be comfortable next to high-profile people.

AYDIN

My house was my sanctuary, and nothing was allowed to interrupt my peace. I'd had my home for over five years. Right after I finished fighting for my country, I bought this property and built it from the ground up. The place was two stories and over five thousand square feet with high ceilings, wooden floors, a long deck, and a pool out back with a grill. There was a gym room outside and a man cave in the basement. Oftentimes, my brothers and Nasir would end up over here to hang out more than they did at the bar; it was more relaxed and set up for a bachelor. I never brought women here because I didn't do relationships. It could be because of the women I'd come across that only wanted me for my status and money. After so many questionable moments of getting asked about marriage when they barely put any effort in getting to know me, I learned quickly to only use them for my needs and not rely on getting any closer.

I slammed the weight down on the bench and wiped the sweat away from my forehead with the back of my hand. I was meeting with Nasir and the guys later to hang out since in their minds, I never did anything fun besides work. The few times we got together, it was mostly at the shooting range or playing ball. They'd come to my parents' house for a few events, but mostly, I stuck to my brothers or Nasir.

Ring!

"Addison, I told you to call me on my office line." I lifted the towel, rubbed the sweat off, placed it around my neck, and headed out of the gym to shower.

"Aydin, please, you like when I call you personally," she cooed through the phone, and I sighed and took a seat in my chair. Addison had tried her best to get my company and me to be right up under her thumb and I'd rejected her at every turn. Her father thought it would be good press if we got together, since I'd done security work for him for many years, but he never told her no. She'd become a spoiled brat who expected everything to be handed to her.

"What do you need, Addison?" I turned the water on and tossed the towel in the side bin next to the door.

"I need a date."

"And?"

I knew she wanted me to be her date for the fundraiser, but I never gave her false hope. It was strictly business, and that was only if I felt like dealing with her. Most times, I passed her off to Nasir.

"Aydin, please. What would it look like if I showed up alone?" she whined. I heard a door shut and walked over to the monitor on the wall in my bathroom to see my brother run to the kitchen. I shook my head and slid the phone between my shoulders.

"Addison, I have to go."

"Wait! What about tomorrow?"

"That's not my problem. I only do security for your father."

"We could be so much more, Aydin."

I blew out an annoyed breath.

"I don't mix business with pleasure."

"You always say that."

"I mean it every time." I removed the phone from my ear, ended the call, and laid it on the counter to step in the shower. I didn't plan on staying out all night because of tomorrow's event. I'd hoped to not deal with Addison's attitude, but from that phone call, she would try me again.

Boom! Boom!

"Hurry up in there!"

I did another lap on my chest, turned the water off, and placed a towel around my waist.

"Get out of my house!" I yelled back at my brother.

"I'm telling Mom!" He chuckled. I grabbed another towel for my face and walked out of the bathroom. Wesley stood with a sandwich in his hand, grinning, and I flipped him off as I opened my closet to grab a shirt and jeans.

"Don't you have a place of your own?" I stepped back in the bathroom.

"Nope. Mom said she was going to let me grab some food later tonight."

"You're a grown man."

He shrugged. I reached to take the plate out of his hand, and he turned away from me.

"Are you coming with us tonight?"

"Yeah, Nasir called and said everyone was meeting up."

Being older now, I didn't mind hanging out with Wesley, but when we were younger, he was the most annoying middle brother. Everything was about him or my younger brother, Josiah. As the oldest, I had to be the protector. Even though at his job he was professional and a kickass police officer, outside of the uniform, he was a big kid. Grabbing my keys and wallet, I headed out of my room toward the front door to leave.

"You're driving," Wesley demanded and slid to the passenger-side door.

"Don't get fucked up tonight. I'll leave your ass." I climbed in the car.

"I promise to not get wasted." He held up two fingers close to his heart.

"You're lying."

He wiggled his brows.

"What's up with the senator's daughter?"

"What are you talking about?"

"I'm working the event tomorrow."

"Why didn't you tell me?" I stopped at the stop sign.

He shrugged and turned the radio on.

"I forgot."

"She called before you came over."

"You sure you never slept with her?"

"Hell no." I drove into traffic, listening to him spill about the gossip going on about Addison and her family's name.

Thirty minutes later, we arrived at the bar. I stepped out of the car with Wesley already flirting with some girls who walked in front of us. He held the door open, and they thanked him and giggled in his face. I noticed Nasir and Nicco near the pool table in the back corner; I strolled toward them and nodded to the bartender.

"Usual, Aydin!" he called out.

"Thanks, B."

Brian's worked at Good Fox for about two years.

"The king has finally arrived." Nicco bowed down in front of me, and I flipped him off.

"How long have you two been here?" I shook hands with Nasir, Nicco, Carter, and a few other guys.

"About thirty minutes," Nasir explained.

The waitress brought over our drinks, and I took a sip right away.

"Are we all set for tomorrow?" Nasir asked.

"Yeah, it should be an easy night."

Nicco set up another round on the table and passed a pool stick toward me.

"We should have the entire place on lock with no issues."

I watched Nicco take the first shot, walked to the right side of him, and took the next shot.

"Isn't that the new assistant at the office?" Carter tapped me on the shoulder. I glanced up and saw Amelia laughing with some guy, and two others. His hand lingered on the lower left side of her back, and my hand gripped the pool stick tighter.

"That's her," Nicco answered.

Amelia smiled at something he whispered in her ear. The four of them went to sit in a booth near the bar.

"Maybe we should invite them over here," Nicco said.

"No," I said.

"Why not?"

"It's your turn."

"Amelia!" Nasir yelled across the room, and I groaned, rubbing a hand down my face. Our eyes met, and I felt her body stiffen when I glared at them. Her friend pointed at us, and she stood and walked over to us. The guy she was with followed her.

"Who's your friend, Amelia?" Nicco asked, and I hit him on the chest.

"Hi guys. I didn't know you'd be here." Amelia ignored his question.

"We like to unwind after a long week," Nasir stated and took the pool stick out of Nicco's hand.

"You should join us," Nicco pressed, and Carter chuckled.

"She's on a date," I answered for her.

"No, I'm not."

"Amelia." The guy placed his hand on her waist.

She peered up at him, blushed, and pushed a piece of her hair behind her ear.

"David, these are my new co-workers at the security firm."

"David, you play pool?" Nasir probed, and I grunted, gawking at Amelia for another second. The guys liked to fuck with new people, especially when it dealt with the women in our company.

"Not really," David answered and slid his hands in his pockets. He seemed like a corporate type with his suit and tie, while everybody else was dressed more casual in jeans and t-shirts.

"I need to get going," I said and placed the pool stick on the table.

"Seriously, we're in the middle of a game!" Nicco groaned, and I shrugged, stepping around Amelia and her date. Before I could leave, she grabbed my arm to stop me.

"Mr. Reeve," Amelia spoke slowly, and I turned to face her.

"Yeah."

"David, can you order me a drink, and I'll meet you at the table," she informed her date.

He looked skeptical, then leaned down to kiss her cheek and walked over to the bar, keeping an eye on us.

"I wanted to thank you again for hiring me. I know you probably didn't want to fight with Molly." She chuckled.

"Don't worry about it."

"Did I do something wrong?"

"No, why do you ask?" I crossed my arms over my chest.

"You just seem standoffish with me. Everyone else has been open and warm to the idea of me working at the firm."

I narrowed my brows.

"I'm not in the business of throwing parties for new hires."

She looked taken aback at my answer.

"I don't expect a party, but a simple good morning would do." Our eyes locked in a standoff.

"Amelia, are you ready?" Her date approached and held her drink up.

Amelia glanced at the drink and back up to him.

"I'm ready," she answered, walking around me. Her perfume danced In her wake, causing a reaction I hated to have.

"You should probably try to handle your mood a little better around her before she figures it out." Nasir tapped me on the arm.

"There's nothing to figure out, Nasir."

"Tell that lie to someone who hasn't worked alongside you for years." Nasir grinned, and we shook hands. I left to go home and rest before the fundraiser tomorrow.

* * *

SUNDAY.

The band played as guests mingled around and talked amongst themselves. Addison flirted with the men to not only get money, but to make me jealous. Plenty of times, I'd told her that it was a lost cause. I never dated clients, especially ones who were corrupt and would do anything to get their names in the media for good or bad reasons.

"Nicco, check in with the team in the kitchen," I spoke into my mic, keeping my eyes trained on the crowd growing in size. Addison rented out the grand ballroom at the Peabody Hotel in downtown Memphis. Close to two thousand in attendance, and we made sure to have the front and back entrances covered with our people. The local police required everyone to have ID before coming and going from the hotel, and Wesley coordinated everything on that side.

"Tell me, Addison, is this your date?" an older woman pried into her business, and I kept my ear to the conversation, focusing more on the people entering the ballroom.

"He's my bodyguard, and his entire team does security work for my family." Addison leaned into me, and I moved back and cleared my throat.

"Would you excuse me?" I turned and whispered in Nasir's ear to watch Addison.

"Where are you going?" Addison questioned, grabbing my elbow.

I noticed Amelia walk in with David, dressed in a ball gown.

"I need to check on something." I inspected her hand on my arm, and she removed it a second later. I stalked over to Amelia and her date to talk to Jimmy when I approached.

"Hey, boss, look who showed up." Jimmy pointed at Amelia.

"Dennis, you don't mind if I talk to Amelia, do you?"

"It's David," he replied, and I ignored him, reaching for Amelia's hand, and walked off to have privacy.

"Mr. Reeve!" She clenched her hands at her sides.

"I told you to call me Aydin."

"But, sir."

I looked in the vacant hall, pushed the first door I saw open, and pulled her inside, then locked it for privacy.

"I told Nasir not to invite you here."

"I… I…" she stuttered.

"What are you doing with him?"

"Mr.—" The words half-died in her throat.

I held my hand to stop her from continuing.

"It's Aydin." I let my gaze wander slowly down her body.

"Aydin, I thought it would be fine to bring a plus one"

"Stay out of my way."

"Nasir said it would be a good thing for me to come to get a hang of things."

"I don't have time to watch you and my client."

"I'm a big girl. I think I can handle myself."

Her eyes stared back at me, and I felt an overwhelming guilt that I'd ignored her since she started at the office, but I knew deep down it wasn't good to have these types of thoughts.

"You couldn't even handle a mugging." I caught myself before I went further, but the damage was already done.

Knock! Knock!

"Aydin! Aydin!" Addison shouted through the door. I reached out, unlocked the door to a red-faced Addison, and Nasir smirking behind her.

"What do you need, Addison?"

"Why are you in the office with this woman?" Addison tried to step inside. I blocked her with my hand.

"I need to get back to my date." Amelia blurted out, and I wanted to punch Nasir in the face.

"Addison, I'll be out in a minute. Amelia, you stay." I tried to close the door, and Addison stuck her foot out to block me.

"I didn't pay to have someone else guard me tonight!

We need to talk about our relationship," Addison said, and I tightened my fist on the doorknob.

"Nasir, take Addison back to the party. We'll talk later," I told her and closed the door.

"What's your problem with me exactly?" Amelia pressed her lips together in a hard line, cocking her head to the left. The dress she wore showed her voluptuous figure, and that ticked me off more, that he was able to get all of her yesterday and tonight.

"You're fired," I blurted out.

"What!"

The first thing that came to mind was to pull her into my arms and plant a kiss on her plump lips that screamed to be sucked on all night long. Her beige, off-the-shoulder dress, revealing her perky breasts, caused my dick to stiffen.

"You're fired."

"You are crazy!"

"Maybe, but I need you to leave."

"I didn't do anything."

Knock! Knock!

"Arghh!" I groaned and reached for the door, and it was her date.

"Amelia, are you all right?" he questioned, and she scowled at me, picked up her purse, and stormed out of the office. I went to follow her, and he stepped in front of me.

"Look, I don't know what's happening, but Amelia is spoken for."

I looked at his hand on my chest and back up to his eyes and glared.

"She works for me."

"That may be true, but you've had two conversations alone with her, and she's been off each time when I try to talk to her."

"Maybe you should worry about yourself."

"Aye! Amelia's pissed off and said you fired her." Nasir stepped in the hallway, and David turned and went toward Amelia.

"Find someone else."

"Aydin, you sound stupid. She's great, and she's fired?"

"Who's the owner?"

"You, but that doesn't mean anything," he said, one side of his mouth twisted into a smile.

"How?"

"Everyone always comes to me after you've fired them, or need something and you say no."

"Wait. How long has this been going on with you undermining me?" My brows drew together in a frown.

Nasir gestured, his hand in the air.

"Ever since we opened TN Security." He smirked.

"You're an ass."

We started to stroll back to the party.

"For you to say that means a lot. But seriously, ease up on her."

I blew out a breath.

"You're right." I felt as if every single muscle in my body was on fire.

"I know I am."

"Where did she go?" I asked her date.

"She needed to use the restroom," David answered.

"All right, when she comes out, tell her I need to speak with her."

"She doesn't want to talk to you."

"David, right? Look, you're trying to protect Amelia, but you don't have to worry about her with him." He didn't like Nasir's statement, and the hard grimace across his face gave away the attitude, so we left him alone to continue monitoring the scene.

"Where's Addison?" Nasir probed.

Nasir and I looked around the room.

"She knows not to leave without one of us." I eased through the crowd and talked to more of my men, and Jimmy pointed to the bathroom.

"Thanks."

"After tonight, Addison and her family will have to find another security team," I stated and watched her father get on the stage to give a speech.

"Ladies and gentlemen, thank you for coming tonight. My daughter is determined to work for the people, and her goals align with mine." Senator Edgar talked to the crowd, and they applauded.

"How much do you think he's stealing from them?" Nasir challenged, and I knew they were corrupt, but I didn't get too involved in their business affairs.

"There's Amelia leaving with her date," Jimmy discreetly spoke into his mic and I looked up and saw her hold hands with him, strolling out of the ballroom.

"Aydin! You've been ignoring me all night long." Addison planted her hand on my chest, and I could tell she was a little tipsy.

"Addison! Come up here, dear," Senator Edgar said.

I removed her hand from my chest, and Addison strolled over to the stage to take the mic from her dad.

"I can never live up to my father's legacy, but I want to make sure I put in a good fight!"

The audience cheered and clapped.

"I'm running for an open seat in Chicago, and I would do my best to make you proud and continue the legacy of the Chatsworth name." Addison hugged her father, and the crowd loved each moment.

Thirty minutes earlier.

"What do you mean he fired you?" Dani inquired, and I paced the bathroom in frustration.

Aydin fired me, and I hadn't even been there a month to even mess anything up.

"He pulled me into some office and told me I'm fired." I picked up the napkin off the counter and dabbled tears away before they fell.

"Calm down. Where are you?"

"In the bathroom of the ballroom."

"Maybe you misunderstood what he said."

I raised my hand up in the air.

"How can you misunderstand getting fired, Dani?"

"Did you say something to him? I remember things looked intense at the bar yesterday."

"No, I mean it mostly was about why he's been so cold toward me."

"That couldn't have pushed him to fire you though."

I dropped the tissue in the trash, checked my makeup in the mirror, and listened to Dani ramble about how I should go back and beg for my job back.

"I'm about to go home and sleep this night away."

"Well, is everything going well with David?"

"Things are fine, but he's not my type."

"Give it time, Amelia. You always drop a guy fast without giving them a chance."

"We'll see." I ended the call, dropped the phone in my purse, and walked down the hall toward the ballroom. Then I heard a loud slap.

"Get your shit together! What am I paying you for?" I overheard a familiar voice.

I looked behind me and then forward to see if anyone was coming, leaning in closer to the closed door.

"You paid me to do a job. I'm not killing anyone," a deep voice replied.

"Unless I get this position, you won't see the light of day in jail."

"The numbers can't be faked, Addison!" he shouted.

I gasped, ran away from the hallway, and bumped into a hard chest.

"Sorry." I stepped out of his hold and headed through the crowd. I looked back, and his eyes narrowed on me while I focused on picking up my jacket. Then David approached me at the door.

"Hey, you all right?" David helped me into my coat.

"I'm not feeling well."

"Let me grab my ticket for my car."

"I'm sorry for bailing on you." We left the ballroom, our hands locked together, and headed toward the front entrance of the hotel.

"Do you want to get something to eat? Maybe I can save this date." He nudged his shoulder into mine. The car arrived, and the valet passed him the keys and opened the door to let me climb in. David felt more like a friend. Even though Dani and his friend were dating, it didn't mean we'd be a match. This being the second date put in perspective after he mostly talked about his past dating experiences and the type of woman he wanted for marriage. This was my time to get back on my feet, and marriage was a long way from being a priority for me. After we arrived home, David walked me to my apartment, and I hugged him good night and slid my key in the door.

"This is insane," I muttered.

* * *

THE NEXT DAY, I stormed into the office and walked up to Nasir's door without an announcement.

"Nasir, I need to talk to you," I blurted out and quickly regretted the intrusion when I saw he had a girl sitting in his lap. I covered my eyes and turned to walk out of the office. "I'm so sorry," I apologized, treading to the door.

He chuckled.

"You're fine, Amelia. We're decent. What's going on?"

"Are you sure? I can come back." I paused for a breath.

"I thought we were having breakfast together." Her nose took a scornful tilt.

"Not this time. I'll call you about dinner." Nasir kissed her on the cheek, and she rolled her eyes and snarled at me while walking out.

"So sorry about this, but I couldn't wait."

"You're not fired." Nasir leaned on the edge of the desk.

"How did you know that's what I was going to ask?"

"I know Aydin." His mouth jerked into a grin.

"What's his deal?"

"Once you get to know him, things will smooth out."

"Are you sure I won't get fired again if he sees me?"

"He won't. I promise." Nasir stood and headed around his desk to take a seat. I stepped closer to the desk.

"There's something else I need to talk to you about."

"Go ahead," he said, his voice firm as a rock.

"How long has Addison Chatsworth been a client?" My voice shook slightly.

"A while. Is something wrong?" He placed his pen down on the desk and focused on me.

"Well, I'm not sure, or maybe I'm thinking too much into things."

"Have a seat and start from the beginning."

"I think Addison Chatsworth is about to steal the election."

"How do you know that?"

"I overheard her talking about killing someone."

"Hold up! Addison Chatsworth, the daughter of Edgar Chatsworth?"

"I know it seems crazy, but I heard it really clear."

"You heard, but did you see?" He raised a brow.

I sat back in the seat, dropped my shoulders, and knew then he wouldn't believe me.

"The door was closed, but—"

I was cut off when he raised his hand.

"Listen, Amelia, I think you're doing a great job, but unless you have proof, it would be hard to bring this to Aydin."

"There was a guy there too."

"Do you know if they saw you?"

"I doubt it, because I left right after I heard the words kill."

He rubbed a hand down his face as someone knocked on the door.

"It's open!" Nasir yelled out, and I turned to see Aydin open and close the door.

"Just ignore what I told you." I stood and started to leave his office.

"Wait! I want to apologize to you." Aydin reached out to stop me. I peered at his hand on my wrist and back up to his eyes. He took a step back to put space between us.

"For firing me?" I quizzed.

"Nasir brought it to my attention I was being too hard on you."

"The correct term was asshole," Nasir rushed to say, and Aydin moved toward him, and Nasir held his hands up to surrender.

"I was wrong, and you're not fired," Aydin bluntly replied and hoped I got the hint.

"Thank you. I need to get back to work." I went to leave.

"There's something else you forgot," Nasir said.

"It can wait," I answered.

"No, it can't, especially if what you heard is true." Nasir rose out of his seat.

Aydin looked from Nasir to me.

"Should I be filled in on this conversation?" His brows sank into a scowl.

"He didn't believe it, so I doubt you will." I was going to figure out Addison's situation on my own.

"Let me decide before you just assume." Aydin waited for me to speak. I let out a long-held breath, shut the door behind me, and replayed the conversation I heard to Aydin.

"I didn't see, but I remembered her voice from earlier."

Both men looked at me blankly.

"So, you heard her say kill."

"Yes, and some guy told her he wouldn't go that far."

"And you never saw either of them?"

"You don't have to pretend. If you don't believe me, that's fine." I crossed my arms under my breasts.

"I told her that we'd need more information before we

could do anything. She never saw their faces," Nasir explained, giving his same thoughts from earlier.

"See, you don't believe it. She's a long-time client, and I'm new. Understandable."

I threw my hands up and turned to head back to my office, but I stopped in my tracks when I saw Addison sitting at my desk.

"Hello." I strolled to my desk, and she sat back and smiled.

"Amelia Edwards." Addison stood and extended a hand for a shake.

"And you're Addison Chatsworth. We've met." Her smirk fell, and she stepped around me to grab a pen off my desk. Addison came across very spoiled and entitled, that we should all bow down and give into anything she wants.

She tapped the pen on the desk.

"That's right, I caught you in the office with my boyfriend."

"Boyfriend. Who's your boyfriend?"

"Aydin. Did I not make it clear last night?" She sat in the chair in front of my desk. Aydin made it clear he wasn't in a relationship, especially with her.

"You did, but is there something you needed specifically?"

"I wanted to find out if you enjoyed the fundraiser last night."

"It was interesting."

"Interesting. That word is something I've never heard about my events." She nodded, watching me with a long-held eye contact. I couldn't help but think she was here to find out what I heard; something about her surprise pop-up was questionable.

"It was my first time, so I don't have anything to compare it to."

"True." She rubbed her hand up her thigh, then stood.

My eyes peered up at her.

"Aydin told me you're the office manager or something, so I wanted to bring you the check for last night's event." Addison pulled a check from her purse and extended it to me.

"You could have left this with the front desk."

"I could have, but I wanted to meet you and apologize for my attitude last night."

"Forgiven, nothing to bring up anymore."

I flipped open my file folder to start work.

"That's a check for ten thousand, and I wanted to book another event in Chicago."

"I would have to speak with Aydin."

"What does that mean?"

"Molly handles most of the bookings, and she's out on vacation." I logged into my computer and pulled up the calendar of accounts we handled.

"I'm sure Aydin would tell you to just put me in for next month."

"I would suggest you take that up with him."

She glared at me.

"Of course, ohh… there's one more thing." she started to leave, raised her hand, and my leg shook in nervousness.

"Uh huh."

"I hope my speech moved you to make a donation." She winked and walked out of my office. I rubbed the back of my neck and down my face.

"She knows," I muttered to myself. I dove into work and brought up the contracts they had with Addison's family, remembering the numbers didn't look right from the last two events they provided for her family.

Ring!

"Amelia Edwards," I answered and checked through my emails.

"I take it you still have a job."

I chuckled at Dani's comment, leaned back in my seat, and crossed my legs.

"I barged into Nasir's office and told him about me being fired."

"Nasir. That name sounds sexy," Dani teased.

"Nope, you have enough men on your roster."

"Ughh, stop trying to block me."

"I'm saving you." I cackled on the phone.

"So, what happened with your boss?"

"He apologized, and I came back to my office to do some work."

"That's it?" she challenged me. I didn't make it my business to try to understand Aydin, but everyone else at my job was cool, and I was able to get back on my feet already and get my living situation squared away.

"What are you calling me for, Dani?" Normally, she'd be deep into work and not answering her phone, but something changed. I was the one she chose to bug during the middle of the day.

"I called to see if you wanted to have lunch today."

Dani worked as a manager of a jewelry store not too far from me, and she'd been there for six years. Recently, they wanted to promote her to regional manager, but she hadn't decided because that would mean more responsibility and less time for her dating life.

"Not today. I have too much to catch up on." She would want to have lunch. Then shopping, and I had a schedule compared to her being a manager.

"Boring. Well, call me later if you're free."

She ended the call, and I went back into my reports on Addison. Most of the checks came from the same bank except one showed Bank of Chicago. I ran through the other paperwork and noticed everything was filed with one of the accountants at the office named Tristan.

"Tristan," I muttered and rose out of my seat to speak with him. By the end of the day, I wanted to have enough information to bring to Nasir, and he could decide if Aydin should know what was going on with the Chatsworths' organization. As I walked down the hallway, I heard laughter from Nicco's office and waved at him and Nasir. After I made it to the elevator, I pushed the button for the sixth floor for the accounting department and recounted in my head how I would approach Tristan. People didn't like to be accused of anything, and I knew I'd freak out and be ready to fight. The doors came open. I waved at some of the staff, and I looked at each door to find Tristan's name. The door was closed. I tapped lightly on the door when it was opened suddenly, and Addison came out.

"Funny we meet again so soon." Addison pulled her jacket up on her shoulder, as a man came up behind her, and I assumed he was Tristan.

"Addison, you were leaving," he said, and I felt a chill go down my back. The deep, raspy voice was familiar.

"Tristan, call me later. Amelia, we'll talk soon." Addison headed to the elevator.

"Amelia, did you need something?" Tristan questioned.

"No, sorry. I had the wrong door."

"Are you sure?"

I held my hands up and motioned him off.

"Positive, I had the wrong office. Still trying to learn my way around here," I joked and went back to the elevator. I hit the button, looked over my shoulder, and saw him stare at me. I waved when the doors opened and went back to my office. I jumped on my computer and typed in Addison's website. I located her staff and the address of her

Chicago and Tennessee locations. I picked up my phone and dialed the number on the website.

"Offices of Addison Chatsworth."

I cleared my throat.

"Hello, I'm from…"

"Yes."

"Yes, sorry, I'm from Channel Seven News, Kelly Rose."

"How can we help you?"

"Our station was impressed with Miss Chatsworth's recent campaign event."

"Happy to hear that. Love when we make an impact."

"I'd hoped to get more information on Addison's campaign pledge total."

"We reported all of our numbers."

"Interesting, I'm a huge fan of Addison Chatsworth and wanted to make a pledge."

My stomach felt queasy at the lie that rolled off my tongue.

"All pledges are welcome, and you can go to our website."

"Do you mind if I sent one to her personally? I mean with us both in the public eye…"

"I understand. If you're interested, she has multiple businesses you could donate."

"That would be wonderful if I could get a list of them."

"Sure, no problem."

As the assistant recalled each company, I made a note on a piece of paper to research each one and the finances to match up against what she paid to the security firm. By the time she'd finished, I had five companies that looked legit online, but I knew it could be a front. I needed to rethink what I was doing and get some help before I ended up getting fired again.

AYDIN

$\mathcal{A}$ week later.

Nicco and Nasir bitched about me, along with my brothers, about the game. I let out one last breath and rubbed my palm over my face. I invited everyone over to hang out because we didn't have any events to monitor. The office was closed today, and I told Nasir to give everyone the day off paid. Somehow, that included him driving some of my employees to my house. He knew I hated people in my space, but anything I said got ignored unless I put my foot down.

"Block!" Josiah yelled, jumping up from the couch.

"Don't spill that beer on my floor, J," I complained, coming around from the kitchen and passing a bottle to Nicco.

"I have a hundred bucks on this game," Josiah groaned. Wesley laughed because we all knew Josiah never could pick a winning team. He loved the Eagles, and we went for the Titans as our home team. Often, we'd take our dad to games, but we'd missed the latest game because of work.

"You never win anyway," Wesley joked, and Josiah popped him in the arm.

"Aye! Take that outside," I told them, and they laughed at me.

"You sound like Dad," Josiah replied, and I flipped him off.

"Better Dad than Mom." Wesley joined in on the fun.

"Leave my wife out of your grip." Dad picked up another slice of pizza.

"Mom would have knocked them both upside the head."

"True," Josiah and Wesley spoke at the same time.

"Did you talk to Amelia lately?" Nasir brought up.

"No, we see each other in passing."

I grabbed a plate and piled on two slices of pizza and wings.

"She pretty much avoids me now," Nasir said, and I thought about our last conversation in his office. It wasn't on purpose that I avoided her, but when it came to my work, that was my focus.

"Amelia's sexy. Is she dating anyone?" Josiah whispered to Wesley.

"She's off-limits."

"Says who?" Wesley wondered.

"Me," I demanded.

"See how he treats us." Josiah motioned from Dad to me.

"Who's Amelia?" Dad asked.

"No one."

"His new assistant," Josiah explained and started to describe her, but I smacked him on the back of the head.

"Ouch!" Josiah spilled some of his beer.

"Keep her name out of your mouth."

"You must like her." Josiah wiggled his brows.

"No, she works with us, and that means you respect her and any woman who works at the office."

"He's in love."

"Shut up."

"Maybe we were too hard on her about Addison." Nasir sighed.

"What happened with her and Addison?" Wesley questioned.

"She thought something was funny with Addison," Nasir said.

"Funny how?" Everyone's attention was pulled to Nasir because he didn't dive deep into the issue at the office.

"She thought she overheard Addison say something about killing someone."

"Come again?" My mouth went dry at the statement.

"I wanted her to talk to you, but I guess she decided to keep it to herself," Nasir replied, and I placed the beer on the table.

"Start from the beginning."

"Addison Chatsworth killed someone." Wesley looked at Nasir.

"Come to my office." I waved for Nasir to follow me to the back, nudged the door open for him to step in, and motioned to close it behind him.

"What happened between Addison and Amelia?"

"As far as I know, Amelia might have overheard Addison discussing killing someone."

"We both know Addison wouldn't hurt a fly."

"Do we?"

"What's that supposed to mean?"

"Her family has ties into a lot of things, and we've only seen the surface."

I rubbed my chin and sat in thought.

"Have you looked into what she said?"

"Not really. I'd hoped she'd tell you, because I said not to discuss it with you unless she had real evidence." He held a regretful look across his face.

"We can't accuse Addison of something without proof."

"You believe her?"

"Who?"

"Amelia." He smirked, and I sat against the desk.

"Get your mind on the issue."

"She did run out of the event fast that night."

"I need real proof. Addison would bullshit her way out of anything. Then her father would put my business in a bad light."

"Another way is to look at the camera from that night."

"We only have the angle of the ballroom."

"Talk to the hotel manager for the hallway angles."

"Let me think it over first."

"What are you going to do in the meantime?"

I lifted the phone and dialed Amelia's number.

"Talk to Amelia."

"Maybe I should be there."

"I'm capable of being professional."

"Somehow it doesn't come across that way when it pertains to her."

"This is business."

I heard her voicemail message.

"*You can leave a message.*" I hung up and stood.

"No answer."

I shook my head.

"Her voicemail."

"She's probably out on a date again." He chuckled, and I grunted to avoid a conversation on her dating life.

"I'll be back." I reached in my pocket to grab my keys.

"Where are you going?"

Nasir walked out of my office behind me.

"To her place."

"Not sure that's a good idea."

I turned to face him.

"Why?"

"It's the weekend and more than likely, she's out with friends."

"Come with me."

"You have guests here."

"They'll be fine." I went to grab my jacket, and my brothers stopped their conversation.

"What's going on?"

"He's going to Amelia's place."

"I'm tagging with you." Josiah jumped from the loveseat, and I groaned in frustration.

"I can handle this by myself."

"More than likely, you'll be calling one of us to bail you out." Wesley stood, along with Nicco.

"See, you need backup," Nasir pushed, and I knew he was right, but Amelia wouldn't like for everyone to show up at her place unannounced. Saturday afternoon was my time to relax. I could assume she turned her phone off and wanted to be away from anything that had to do with business.

* * *

AN HOUR LATER, I pulled up to her building and parked with Nasir about to push the door open to follow me up the stairs.

"When we get up there, let me do all the talking. You two stay in the car." I pointed at all of them. The best chance for us not to cause her to get pissed off was to not have five big guys break down her door. I walked into the lobby of her building and headed toward the elevator and called for her floor. As we stepped on, I bumped into another guy, and he kept walking and ignored me.

"Prick."

Nasir pushed the button for her floor, and I stood to the side and focused on how I would approach her about Addison. A few seconds later, we stepped off and approached her door, raising my hand to knock.

"Wait! Look at this," Nasir said, pointing to the door cracked open.

"Hey! What are you guys doing?" a loud, squeaky voice interrupted us. Nasir and I glanced at the older woman. She was about five-two in height, probably around her late seventies with rollers in her hair and wearing a housecoat.

"Do you know if Amelia is home?" Nasir probed, and I let him continue in conversation as I moved forward in the apartment and looked around. From the living room, nothing stood out, and Nicco went to the kitchen. I held my gun in my hand.

"She said Amelia left earlier this morning." I heard Nasir behind me from the bathroom.

"I don't see Amelia leaving her door open like this."

"I agree with you. Did you check her bedroom?" Nasir's voice trailed off. He strolled to the other end of the apartment. I gazed at the pictures on the walls of her as a little child with her parents, then shifted toward the closet on the right, and checked around. Nothing showed anything was stolen, so more than likely, she forgot to lock up behind her. I gathered in the living room with Nicco, as Nasir met up front a few seconds later.

"Anything?"

"Spotless," Nasir replied, and we had no doubt Amelia wouldn't call the police if she were in trouble.

"Um... Hello, did I miss the invite?" All three of us turned around at the smooth voice and saw the woman who was with Amelia at the bar with her date. Right behind her, the door opened further, and Amelia came in with her eyes popped wide open with bags in her hands.

"Amelia."

"Why are you guys in my apartment?" Amelia set her bags on the couch and approached us.

Her floral perfume rested under my nose, and I took a step back to give us space before I crossed that line.

"Aydin wanted to talk to you about Addison. We came and saw your door was open."

Nasir explained and left out any mention of contacting me by phone first.

"It couldn't wait until I was at work?" Amelia's spicy personality surfaced, and she wasn't this quiet, go with the flow type of girl.

"Not when it has to do with my business."

"Are you going to introduce me to your friend, Amelia?" Her friend reached her hand out to Nicco and Nasir, and I finally removed my eyes from Amelia and shook her hand.

"This is Nicco, Nasir, and my boss Mr. Reeve. My best friend Dani Phillips," Amelia answered and once again, she dismissed me, avoiding eye contact.

"It's Aydin."

"Aydin." She glanced over her shoulder at Amelia.

"What can I do for you?" Amelia sucked in her breath.

"Tell me the exact words Addison used."

Amelia peered at Nasir, and he nodded at her to answer. I didn't like how she was so comfortable with him, but I knew Nasir thought of her as a friend.

"After we left the bathroom, I happened to walk by and overhear Addison's voice."

"Anyone else? Think hard. I need to be sure of what my next move will be."

"I'm positive it was a guy in the room with her."

"She told me they said something about killing and money," Nasir finished.

"What money?" I needed enough evidence before I talked to Edgar about his daughter. They'd been a long-time client and respected in the community and world.

"I think the money is from the security firm."

"Tell me."

Amelia walked over to the coffee table, picked up her laptop, sat on the couch, and pulled up a document.

"Remember when I said some numbers were off from your payments?" She looked intently at me, and I confirmed with a nod.

"I believe she's working with someone in the security firm to skew the numbers of payments."

"Why?"

I didn't doubt her, but what was Addison's goal?

"Through her donation and campaign events, she's cooked the books, and the people she hires have no idea the way she's moving the money around through her checks." Amelia spoke with a scroll of each event we'd covered for her and the Chatsworth family throughout the years.

"I need to talk to her."

"That shouldn't be a problem. When you call, she runs," Amelia mumbled under her breath.

I heard her friend giggling under her breath.

"The last thing I heard she's in Chicago."

"All right, go to Chicago. Amelia, you'll have protection until we figure everything out."

"That's not necessary."

She closed her laptop.

"As far as Addison is concerned, she might not have you on her radar, but I can't take that chance."

"You're overreacting." Amelia jumped off the couch.

"Maybe he's right, Amelia," Dani agreed.

"They didn't see me."

"How do you know? What happened for you to leave so abruptly?"

"After she threatened to kill someone, I just ran, and some guy helped me after I almost fell."

"Some guy?" My brow raised in confusion.

"Yeah."

"You didn't say anything to me that someone saw you." Nasir and I made eye contact.

She fidgeted with her hands.

"I mean I didn't think it was serious. He didn't say anything."

I ran a hand through my hair, blowing out a frustrated breath.

"How did he look?"

Nicco pulled out his phone.

"Um… probably around five-nine, dark hair, a small scar on his cheek, and a tattoo that was covered on his neck."

"I'll look into her database for any descriptions." Nicco dialed our team back at the office.

"You're coming to stay with me, Amelia," Dani said.

"I'll be fine," Amelia assured her.

"Someone could have given Addison a heads-up," Nasir suggested, and I rubbed my cheek in thought.

"She needs protection."

"I'll be fine," Amelia called out.

"What about your parents, Amelia?" Dani challenged.

"We're going to speak with Addison, but in the meantime, she needs to be watched."

"I'm not some trophy that's delicate and can't protect herself," she fussed.

"Aydin's right, Amelia. You need to have protection, plus your family," Nasir explained, and I knew what I was about to say would put me in an awkward situation.

"She'll stay with me."

All eyes looked at me.

"What!" she shouted.

"You'll stay with me. Your apartment isn't safe."

"That's not needed, Aydin."

"You'll be under twenty-four hours of protection until we figure out what Addison is planning, plus your parents."

"No."

"No?"

"I can protect myself and my family."

"Amelia." Dani watched as Amelia marched out of the living room.

"Talk to her."

"I'll try," Dani said.

AMELIA

*T*wo days later.

Aydin had no clue who Addison was after, but I'd been fine with no supervision for the past thirty-five years of my life and didn't need a babysitter now. Right now, I was on my way to my parents' home for dinner and planned on keeping my routine the same. I'd sent Nasir all the information I had found, got the locksmith to add double locks to my apartment, and spoke with the apartment building about anyone coming and going who asked about me. Everyone was overreacting that Addison wanted to hurt me. She was too far into appearances and if her reputation came across that she was involved in something illegal, the entire family would have put a stop to her dealings. Scandal in politics wasn't a good look. After I parked, I unlocked the door and waved at my mom's neighbor Mrs. Winters. The entire Winters family was close to our family and watched me when I was younger. Plus, I played with their daughter in middle school before she moved out of state after high school.

I knocked on the door, and Mom opened it with a

phone up to her ear as usual. She reached out for a hug, and I shut the door behind me.

"Who are you gossiping with?"

"Dani."

I rolled my eyes.

"Tell her to stay out of my business please."

"All right, Dani. Let me call you back."

I followed her to the couch and sat. I pushed my purse on the table and slipped out of my shoes. Cassandra Edwards worked at the postal office, and my dad worked for a grocery store in the executive department. He'd been there before I even was born and started out as a bagboy.

"Where's Dad?" I removed my jacket.

"On his way home."

"What did you cook?"

She studied me.

"Why are you looking at me like that?"

"When were you going to tell us?"

"Tell you what?"

"Amelia, don't play with me, little girl."

"What did Dani tell you?"

"Somebody is trying to kill you."

I chuckled.

"Ma, Dani watches too much *Law and Order.*"

"Then you tell me."

"It's not a big deal."

"Let me and your father worry if we think it's a big deal or not."

"Yes, ma'am."

"Dani said your boss wants you to have protection." She sat next to me on the couch.

"He's overreacting. I overhead something, and I didn't know if it was serious or not."

"Has to be serious if Dani called that you'd been staying

at her place."

"Just for the past two days. I needed to get my locks changed."

"Amelia!" she gasped, grasping my hands.

"Don't worry. My building is secure, and the cameras didn't catch anyone inside the building that looked weird."

"Maybe you should stay here."

"No, it'll blow over soon."

"Well, how is work overall?"

"Work is great, and I love it actually."

Mom released my hands and stood.

"Tell me about it while I finish dinner."

"You remember I told you I work as an operations manager."

"That's a big position. I thought you applied for secretary."

"I did and the office manager, Molly, gave me the position of assistant to the owner and operations manager."

"How is your boss?"

She passed me a grater and a block of cheese. We stood at the counter together and talked.

"Different."

"That sounds like you're annoyed."

"My first day he ignored me practically."

"Ignored like dismissive."

"Basically, and then he fired me."

She stopped before she turned the fish over.

"Fired you, why?"

"Aydin's in his own world. I think he wasn't expecting someone to not buy into his bullshit."

"Listen if he tries you again."

"We've had a talk, and he's apologized. That's why I was surprised when he invited me to stay with him."

"Stay as in his home?"

"Yeah, it surprised everyone." I placed a piece of cheese in my mouth.

"Is he cute?"

"Mom."

"What? Girl, I'm a woman first."

"Men are not in my thought process right now."

She took the cheese and poured it in the red sauce with onions, before transferring it on top of the fish.

"If this job is going to bring you danger, I think you need to look into other work. I'll check at the post office."

"That's the last thing I should do is work alongside my mom."

"Safer at my job."

Mom lifted the plate of fried fish and handed it to me.

"Smothered fish smells good."

Keys in the door dinged, and Dad came in whistling.

"Look at my two favorite women."

"Hi, Dad."

He kissed my mom on the neck and stepped around her to kiss me on the cheek.

"You look pretty, baby."

"Thanks, how was work?"

Dad dropped the mail on the table.

"Long, but happy to be here and ready to eat."

"Go change your clothes and wash up," Mom said.

I grabbed the knife to cut into the fish and placed a small amount on each plate, and Mom set the bread on the table. A few seconds later, he came back to the kitchen and sat.

"Amelia, is everything good with you?"

Mom and I locked eyes.

"Everything is fine."

Mom blurted out an annoyed noise.

."What am I missing?" Dad watched me, and I pushed

food around my plate.

"Nothing, to worry you guys about."

Ring!

My cell phone rang, interrupting me.

"Hello," I answered, pulling my phone from my jacket.

"Your guards are outside."

"Aydin?"

"Don't fight me on this."

"Who told you where I am?" I whispered harshly through the phone.

"I'm in the security business." He ended the call, and I shook my head.

"Everything okay?" Mom questioned.

"I'm going to head to Dani's."

"Who was that on the phone?" Dad asked.

"My boss."

I grabbed the food container and poured enough for me and Dani, put the lid on top, and kissed them both on the cheek.

"Something you need to tell me?" He watched me put the plate in the sink, and I sighed.

"Mom can fill you in after I leave, but I'm okay. I promise."

* * *

TEN MINUTES LATER, I walked out of my parents' house, and when I got in my car, I saw one parked across the street, and they waved at me. All I planned on doing was go out and have dinner with my family and then head home to a nice bubble bath, with a glass of wine. Before I turned off to Dani's apartment, I pulled into Walmart and saw the guards pull up a second later. He started to get out, but I waved him off.

"I'll be fine. I only need to grab a few items. You can stay in the car."

"Our order is to stay with you at all times."

I held my hand up to stop him.

"It's Walmart; there are cameras everywhere."

He gazed down at his watch.

"Ten minutes; if you're not out, we'll come in to get you."

"Deal."

I left them out in the car and walked into the store, lifted the basket and went to the aisle to pick up a few soaps and toothpaste I needed to replenish.

"Ouch... excuse me."

"I apologize. I didn't see you there."

"No problem."

I started to walk off.

"Excuse me, you dropped this." I looked behind my back, and he held a pen out to me.

"That's not mine."

"You sure?" He walked up on me, held it out to me, and smirked.

"Positive." I turned, and he gripped my arm.

"Wait."

"Ummm..."

"Amelia, everything okay?" I peered up at the guard coming toward us, and the guy who bumped into me released his hold on me and strolled away.

"I... I... yeah. Done."

"Who was that?"

"I don't know."

"Did he hurt you?"

"No, it was a misunderstanding." I pushed forward and dropped everything on the conveyor belt to check out.

All the staff was gone for the day, and I stayed to finish adding new client information into the computer. I tried to not make it a habit to be the last person in the building, but in my new position, I wanted to make a big impression. When I was finished, I grabbed my badge and waved to the janitor. Molly was still out for her wedding and was expected back in a few weeks. I debated if I should call her to update her on what had been going on. I slipped onto the elevator and pushed to go down a level to Tristan's office. I saw his door was closed.

I checked the doorknob and saw it was open. Pushing forward, I closed it behind me and shut the blinds. Strolling to the desk, I turned on his personal computer and noticed it wasn't password protected. I went to his search history and noticed a lot of articles on Addison, TN Security, and me. Most of his work was organized alphabetically, and I started to read when the door was nudged open.

"What are you doing in here?" the janitor asked.

Jamal was in his late fifties with a wife and grandkids.

We'd had lunch a few times, and he walked me to my car if I ever worked late.

"I forgot some files with Tristan, and I needed to get them before my meetings." I turned the computer off and rose out of the chair.

"Tristan knows you come in here?"

"He forgot to send me them before he left. You know how you men are."

I laughed, and Jamal chuckled and left the office. I locked the door and released a long-held breath.

Once in my car, security was behind me, and I told them I was taking the freeway to get back to Dani's place faster. I turned the music up, bopping my head when my cell rang. Dani's name scrolled across, and I answered.

"On my way to your place."

"How many nights are you going to work late?"

"Things are busy at the office."

"Sounds like it, and your mom told me to tell you to call her tomorrow."

"When did she call me?"

"Your phone's been off."

"I'm sorry. After my lunch, I needed to focus and catch up on work."

"Security still following you?"

I looked out the side mirror and saw the lights from the car. It looked like they were extremely close, but they probably didn't want anyone to get between us.

"Yes but let me get off this phone so I can concentrate on traffic."

"Be safe and see you soon."

We hung up.

Click!

My car suddenly made a noise, but I was lucky to be close to the off ramp. I put on my turn signal and prepared to get off the freeway when my car stopped. I was able to get it to the side of the road. Rolling my window down, I waved to the security about what was happening. Rory finally told me his name after a week of not speaking because Aydin told them I wasn't to have any conversation beside my schedule of the day. He leaned down in my window.

"Did—"

Pop!

"Ahhhhh!" I screamed at the blood from the hole in his head, removed the seatbelt, and crawled to the passenger side of the car to climb out on my back.

Pop!

I stayed down and looked to see what direction the bullet came from.

"Think… Think."

I decided to jump up and run through the woods because I knew a gas station was on the other side, and I could call the police to come help.

Pop! Popppp!

"Arghhh!" More shots flew over my head. I stood behind a tree to catch my breath and saw a flashlight from behind me. I took off and ran through the woods and across the road toward the gas station and banged on the door.

"Open the door! Please." I screamed, looking behind me. No one followed me.

"We're closed," he yelled.

"Someone's trying to kill me!" I banged on the door again.

Pop! Poppp!

The door unlocked, and I ran in and locked it behind me

"Where's the phone? I need to call the police."

"I don't want any problems," he grunted as he picked up the phone and passed it toward me.

I looked at the door and saw a car turn off its lights.

"He's out there!" I pointed and ran behind the counter and dropped down.

"911, what is your emergency?" the operator picked up.

Breathing heavy, I tried to calm my nerves to get the words out.

"I need the police," I whispered.

Ratt!!!!

"Ahhhhh!" The store's glass window broke from more shots.

The owner fell over the counter with a bullet in him.

"Please help me!"

The phone went dead, and the lights went off.

"Amelia!" I opened my eyes and crawled around the counter at the familiar voice, then I saw Nicco at the door. A few seconds later, police sirens sounded as they pulled into the store and ran into his arms.

"Nicco... someone tried to killed me," I stuttered, and he wrapped his arm around me.

"Shushhh... I'll take you home."

"How did you know I was here?"

"Aydin has contacts at the police station because of his brother and they knew to call the office."

"Where's Aydin?"

"He's still in Chicago."

Nicco helped me out of the store and toward the car. Police ran in along with the paramedics. I couldn't stay to answer questions. Numb to what just happened, I needed to be home, and a part of me wanted to talk to Aydin.

* * *

"MAYBE YOU SHOULD TAKE a day for yourself." Dani sipped on her coffee. I was dressed for work the next day, and she probably thought I was stupid. I planned on locating who was behind trying to kill me.

"I'm fine, Dani."

I bit into the buttered toast and poured more cream in my coffee.

"You're not fine, Amelia. Last night someone wanted to kill you."

"Nicco will be with me today."

"Where's Aydin?"

"Still out in Chicago."

"Maybe you should—"

Knock! Knock!

"Who is that?" Dani put her coffee on the counter and went to answer the door.

"Where is she?" He barged inside. Dani's eyes rose in shock.

I LIFTED my phone and saw I had several missed calls.

"Aydin, I was—"

"Let's go."

"Aydin!" I dropped my phone on the table.

"You're going to my place."

"I thought you were in Chicago."

"I was, and I got the call about two attempts on your life."

"The police are investigating."

He shook his head and grabbed my phone.

"Pack your things."

"I have work" I fussed and stood my ground.

Aydin closed the distance between us.

"Nicco told me what happened, and we're going to do things my way now."

My stomach turned knots.

"Aydin, listen to me."

"Pack your things."

"Won't that look weird, me staying with my boss."

"The last thing I'm worried about is how things look."

"Amelia, listen to him."

"Dani's place is secured. We have the guards."

"No!" He shouted, and I jumped nervously.

"Okay."

He sighed and tried to reach for my hand.

"Amelia… sorry I yelled at you. This is just more complicated than I can explain."

"Sure, Aydin."

An hour later, we pulled in at his home, and he turned the car off.

"Who's here?" I noticed two other cars in the driveway.

"My brother and mom."

"Your mother is here!" My eyes widened in shock.

"I wanted to make sure I had everything you needed, and my brother's a cop."

"This is not how I wanted to meet your family."

"Leave your things here, and I'll bring them in a minute." He opened the door and walked around to the passenger door and held it open.

"Your place looks beautiful."

"You haven't seen it yet."

"Well, from the garden, I can tell you're neat and organized."

He laughed and pushed the door open. I followed him in to see his brother, I assumed, on the couch with a remote in his hand.

"Did you get the camera footage?" Aydin asked, and he lifted the brown folder.

"Not a close ID on the license plate."

"This is Wesley."

I started to drop Aydin's hand, and he hesitated. I looked down and back up, then he released me to sit next to his brother.

"Hi. I'm Amelia."

"Wesley, I apologize now for my brother. He can be a little overbearing."

"Wesley, don't talk about your brother like that." An older woman with long curls and petite shape came from the hallway.

"Amelia, I want you to meet my mom Rebecca Reeve." Aydin introduced us.

I shook her hand.

"How are you, Amelia? Aydin told us what happened."

"Fine, it was pretty scary at the time."

"Completely understand," Rebecca said.

"Did you cook?" Aydin inquired.

"Leftover squash and meatloaf," Rebecca answered.

"Are you hungry?" Aydin wondered.

"No. It's still pretty early."

"You'll stay here until we get the people behind this."

"I need to head to the office."

"You'll have to work from here."

"Huh?"

"You can't leave the house, Amelia."

"Aydin, that's ridiculous."

His nostrils flared.

"What's ridiculous is you going behind my back and keeping something from me."

"I didn't go behind your back."

"I told you the minute something changes to call me."

I turned my head away from him.

"Aydin, let me talk to her," Rebecca jumped in, and I felt a little relief that she understood my side.

"She's not leaving."

"You're not my—"

He glared at me, and I caught myself before I answered.

"Amelia, come to the kitchen." Rebecca rubbed my back.

She stepped in behind me, motioned to take a seat at the island, then turned to open the fridge and removed a jug of water.

"How long have you worked with Aydin?"

Rebecca placed the jug in front of me and grabbed two glasses out of the cabinet.

"Not very long."

"He's my oldest and can be a little stubborn."

"Extremely."

"Here you go." She pushed the glass toward me.

"Thanks." I took a sip.

"You're used to having all the answers."

I shrugged.

"From what Aydin has said, you two met because he stopped you from getting mugged."

I nodded.

"The funny part is that I was coming from drinking at a bar after a long day of applying for jobs."

"Well, we've all been there. Aydin is good at his job."

"I know."

"Then why fight him?"

"He's…"

"Mean?"

"Pretty much. I've never had a boss just ignore me."

"He likes you, talks about how smart you are. The entire situation had him worried."

"I get that and understand as an employee, he wants to protect me."

"More than an employee-boss relationship."

"We've never crossed the line."

"Oh, Amelia. I can see it in your eyes, honey. You and my son are smitten with each other."

"I doubt he thinks of me in that way."

"Avoidance doesn't make it untrue."

"You're married, and I met Josiah at the office."

"He's the baby of the bunch."

"I like Josiah."

"All he does is drive me crazy, but that's a conversation for another day."

I chuckled.

"Work here, relax, and try not to worry. Let Aydin handle what he needs to do to protect you and your family."

"Oh, my gosh. I forgot to call my parents."

"When was the last time you talked to them?"

"Before the shooting."

"Probably worried if they saw it on the news."

"I'd planned on getting a new phone. Everything was left in my car."

"Check with Wesley. He probably can help with the tow truck company."

"Thank you, Rebecca."

"No thanks needed."

Aydin stepped in the kitchen, and Rebecca walked out.

"Are you going to the office now?"

"I'll call you with an update. Wesley is staying here. Plus, we have guards out front."

"I need to get a new phone. My purse was left in the car."

"Give me a few hours, and I can get someone to bring it over before the end of the day."

"Thanks, Aydin."

"You're welcome." He covered my hand with his and lightly squeezed.

A few days prior.

Nasir and I flew into Chicago with a few team members, and the goal was to talk with Addison and figure out what's going on. After I left Tennessee, Amelia promised she would stay with the guard I had put on her to keep an eye on her until we got answers. I talked to Edgar before I left and didn't know if I believed he didn't know what she was up to.

"Aydin, what do I owe for this visit?" Edgar sat in his chair and sipped on his glass of whiskey. I drove alone to his house to have a one-on-one to see if I could get the truth about the entire event that night.

"Have you spoken to Addison?"

He shook his head.

"Not since her announcement, a few text messages. You know a senator is pretty busy."

He tilted his head, crossing a leg over the other.

"I received some disturbing news and wanted to confirm."

"You know Addison better than anyone."

"Your daughter threatened to kill someone."

"Hold up, kill someone? Do you know what you're saying right now?"

"The last event was the final one I would be serving for your family."

"The amount of money we bring to you…"

The door opened, and Addison came in with bags in her hands.

"Aydin, well, isn't this a nice surprise."

"Addison, glad you could come and clear up some things."

Addison placed her bags down and went to her father to kiss him on the cheek.

"I can't stay long. My car is waiting."

"Did you threaten Amelia?"

"Who?" Her face scrunched up.

"Don't play dumb, Addison."

Edgar stood and raised his hands.

"Wait a minute, Adyin. You're in my house. You should show my daughter and me some respect."

"What does she have on you, Edgar?"

"Aydin, I have no clue what you think I've done, but I've been working on my campaign."

Addison pulled out her phone and sat on the couch.

I snatched the phone out of her hand.

"Tristan didn't show up for work yesterday."

"Who?" She leaned her head to the side and tapped her finger on the couch.

"I think you should leave, Aydin."

"I'm not leaving until she comes clean."

"You can look at my phone records and email who I've been dealing with. Tristan is not on the list beyond the payment I sent to the firm," Addison said.

Ring!

"Can I have my phone please?" She held her hand out.

"This isn't over."

She smirked and turned to talk on the phone. I left the house and got in the car with Nasir.

"What did she say?"

"Denied everything."

"Tristan's computer was pulled to get someone to go through his accounts."

Nasir started the car when Addison came out of the house and got in her limo.

"Follow her."

Nasir stayed two cars behind the limo as they drove through traffic.

"Did her father have anything to say?"

"Nothing worth using."

The car pulled over in front of a bank, and the door was opened. Addison stepped out and hugged an older guy.

"Bet you she's trying to get into her account."

"Can you freeze her assets?"

"Let me text Carly."

"The deeper this goes, we might need to call in more help."

"Carly's going to look into her business."

"You have a copy of her upcoming events."

"On her website, it showed she's going to do another fundraiser."

"We might have to crash."

"That's fine with me, as long as I don't have to dress up."

Nasir tapped me on the shoulder.

"Look, she's leaving." He started the car and drove off behind her.

Buzz!

My phone vibrated, and I noticed an incoming call

from Rory, the guard I had to monitor Amelia while I was out of town.

"She's been reluctant for us to be around."

"She has no choice."

"This might not be anything, but a guy bumped into her at Walmart."

"Did you get his license plates?"

"It happened too fast."

"Keep me updated and call Nicco if you need backup."

"Everything all right with Amelia?"

I sighed.

"For now."

The next stop we came up to was a hotel, and Addison got out and headed in Lux Hotel. The limo pulled around to the VIP parking. Nasir and I hopped out, handed the keys to the valet, and went inside to watch her talk to the front desk.

"She could be meeting Tristan."

"We need her room number."

"They won't give us that."

"She hit the seventh floor."

"Wait to see how long she stays."

Nasir went to talk to the front desk. I stood off to the side at the payphone and watched the front entrance.

"They couldn't give me a room number, but I flirted with the desk clerk, and she said Addison has the room for one day."

"Then we wait."

* * *

Six hours later.

The elevator doors opened, and Addison walked out to the lobby and turned in her key. As she talked, the older gentleman we saw from the bank approached her with his arm around her waist.

"We need his name."

I gritted through my teeth. Even though Amelia said the man she bumped into at the hotel was younger, I'd bet money he has something to do with Addison feeling confident.

Addison was escorted to her limo, and they drove off. We hopped back in the car and followed.

* * *

Pop! Pop!

Nasir swerved to avoid hitting another car as shots rang by and almost killed us.

"Fuck! She made us." I groaned, reaching in the glove compartment for my weapon.

Addison's car turned sharply, and Nasir hit the gas to speed up before we lost them.

"You hit!" I shouted.

"No, I'm good. You?"

"Good." I looked in the side mirror and saw a white van speed up.

"Stay on her."

"We left the guys to keep an eye on her father's place." Nasir reminded me. I pulled out my phone and called.

"Boss, nothing happening here." Reggie answered the phone.

"Reggie we're in the middle of a chase, and gunshots were fired." I slid my window down and returned fire.

Pop! Pop Pop!

"Keep your phone on; it will track you," Reggie said. I dropped it on my lap and waited for Nasir to turn again at the next light, then I shot back. Addison's limo hopped on the freeway, and a red Honda swerved in in front of us, and we missed our turn.

"Damn it!" Nasir shouted and got off to the side street. I looked back, and the van was gone. My head leaned back, and I closed my eyes to control my breathing.

"Next time, we'll be ready," Nasir said.

"Let's get to the hotel."

* * *

Two hours later, I was out of the shower, changed, and sat with the team to read over the printed files Carly had uploaded.

"Look at this… twenty thousand from a party thrown by the president of some investment firm." Nasir pushed the papers in my hand.

"Call your contacts."

Ring!

"Hold up, this is Nicco," I said.

"It's pretty late in Tennessee right now," Nasir mentioned, and that had my attention.

"We have a big problem," Nicco said.

"What's wrong?" My heart started to beat fast that something happened to Amelia.

"I'm at a gas station because Amelia called the police for help and they hit me up. Someone shot at her."

I jumped up and paced back and forth.

"Who was it?"

"We don't know, but Rory's dead."

"Shit," I cursed under my breath.

"Her car broke down, and I guess when Rory tried to check, he was shot."

"Where's Amelia?"

"With me, we're on the way to Dani's."

"I'm on my way back."

I finished the call and gripped the phone in my hand.

"What did Nicco say?"

"Someone shot at Amelia."

"What's the chance of that happening, and we get shot at too?"

"Rory's dead." I leaned against the wall with my head down.

"How's Amelia?"

"Shaken up."

"I'll get the pilot on the phone."

After so many years in the business and the people we'd worked for, I had made enough to afford a private plane for times like these when we needed to get to a location fast. Nasir and the rest of the guys packed up the files, and I went into the bedroom to grab my luggage, thankful I didn't unload everything earlier. We'd hoped to be out here for a few days but never expected to be involved in a shoot-out. A knock sounded on the door, and I zipped the bag and tossed it over my shoulder.

"He's ready."

I headed to the door and grabbed my jacket, and we left on the elevator.

* * *

ONCE WE GOT off the plane, we climbed in the car and headed straight to Dani's apartment without going to the office. I checked in with Nicco, and he was in front of Dani's home, waiting to take Amelia to the office. I was pissed when he told me she wanted to go to work.

"You need to calm down before we go there," Nasir suggested.

He'd called ahead and had two trucks waiting for us.

"She's testing my patience."

"Amelia just went through something."

"I know that!" I argued.

The driver arrived, and Nicco stepped out of his car. I started to open my door when Nasir caught my arm.

"Not the time to be yourself. Try to look at it from her perspective."

"She's upstairs." Nicco reached a hand out, and I did the same.

"The camera footage?"

"I sent it to your phone."

I knocked on her door and pulled my phone out of my pocket.

"Who could that be?" The door knob turned.

I heard Amelia's voice.

"Where is she?" I barged inside.

"Aydin!" Dani's eyes rose in shock, I marched in her direction and glared at Amelia.

"Aydin, I was—"

"Lets go." I didn't give her any time to think.

I waved her off.

"I have work," she fussed and stood her ground.

"Pack your things."

She didn't move and I closed the distance between us.

"You're not going to work."

We stood in a stare off, and she finally gave in and headed to pack her things. I planned on keeping her with me until this case was solved.

"Aydin, a little more sensitivity goes a long way," Dani commented, and I paused in thought.

"I'll have my team put someone in front of your house and her parents'."

Amelia came back with her bags, and I grabbed them both and dialed Wesley's number. As I escorted Amelia to the car, she avoided making eye contact and talked to only Nicco.

"You're back in town." A crackling noise came through the phone.

"Wesley, I need you to meet me at my house."

"Everything okay?"

"No." I watched Nicco place her bags in the car, and she climbed in next to Nasir.

"Get me everything you know on the shooting at a gas station, plus some information on Addison."

"Send me the details."

"Coming in soon as I hang up."

"Anything else?"

"Have Mom meet me at my house."

"What did you do?"

I pulled my seatbelt over my lap after climbing in the front seat and looked in the rearview mirror at the back-seat. Amelia turned her head to avoid me.

"I might need some assistance."

"She's pissed, huh?"

"Who?"

"Your girlfriend."

"Bye, Wesley."

The driver waited for Nicco to pull in front, and we headed in the direction of my house, I sat back in my thoughts on how to approach the conversation. The second car we had with us would stay in front of Dani's house until Nicco returned.

*T*hree days later.

Amelia was still locked in the guest bedroom and refused to speak to me, but today would be the last day I allowed this to go on. I picked up the plate of food I'd cooked, walked to her room, and tapped on the door.

"What?"

"I made breakfast."

"Not hungry."

"Amelia, you need to eat."

"I ate already."

"When?"

"While you were working out."

"I'm not talking to you through the door."

I waited for a response, then the knob turned, and she stood dressed in only a large shirt with her thick thighs showing in a pair of boy shorts. Her hair was pulled into a bun in the back, and she had on little makeup, only enhancing her full lips, round cheeks, and oval eyes.

"Where are you going?"

I sat the plate on the dresser and gulped down the last remnants of the coffee.

"To work."

"Amelia, we talked about this."

"You yelled, but no conversation happened." She pouted, plopped down on the bed, and continued with her makeup.

"Until Addison is found, you need to be out of sight. This is the best place for you."

"You've convinced me, but why can't I still go to work? You'll be there."

"Because you'll be a distraction."

"For whom?" She turned to me.

How would I admit I'd grown to like our bickering back and forth? Hell, even when she answered the phone when I called, something about her voice made me want to be in her presence. I couldn't pinpoint the exact moment. Besides, when I tried to fire her, she refused.

"Me."

She stared into my eyes.

"Oh."

"Look, how about a compromise?"

"Okay."

"You can go to the office with me, but we won't stay the full day."

"Why not?"

"I still need to track down Addison, and I'd planned on doing that with you here."

"Then if you need to do that, I won't interrupt. I'll be fine."

"Are you sure?"

"Yeah, I can work from here. Molly's back early, and I'll check in with her."

"All right."

I angled to leave but stopped.

"Do you want to have dinner tonight?"

"Dinner like a date?"

Women usually came easy for me, but she was a puzzle I couldn't figure out but enjoyed learning piece by piece.

"You can call it a date or two people who like to eat food."

She blushed, and that only made me want her even more. I knew with us working together, it would never work out.

Amelia went on to finish her makeup, and I walked out of her room and down to my office and sat at my desk. I logged into the camera system of my home and the office and saw Molly step in and hug a few of the guys. I lifted my phone and dialed her number.

"I wondered when you'd call." Molly placed her bag on the desk and picked up the messages.

"Congrats on the wedding; he's a lucky man."

"Thank you, so what's been going on while I was gone?"

"How much time do you have?" I jested.

"Plenty, we're closing on a house soon, so I can catch up on work before I pack up our apartment," Molly replied.

"Amelia's staying at my place."

"Why?"

"Someone tried to kill her."

"Are you serious?"

I shifted in my seat and stood, looking out the window.

"She came across some stuff she shouldn't have, and Addison is involved."

"Of course Addison is behind everything."

"We went to Chicago, and they tried to take us out."

"Aydin, you can't be serious."

"Very serious."

"What do you need me to do?"

"For now, keep the office running. Amelia's determined to continue her work."

"Really? I'm surprised she hasn't left the country for her sanity."

"Believe me, I tried to get her round-the-clock security at first, and she refused. Then the attempt escalated, and I forced her to stay with me."

"Aydin, you can't treat her like a normal client."

"My mom has already yelled at me about how I went about bringing her here."

"Momma Rebecca is always right." Molly giggled.

"Anyway, cancel my appointments. My only priority is catching Addison and Tristan."

"Tristan?"

"Tristan, our accountant is working with her."

"You've gotta be shitting me."

"I wish."

"I see Nasir and Nicco at the door to leave."

"They're about to come over here so we can regroup."

"Should I come and keep Amelia company?"

"If you think that'll keep her calm."

"I'll cancel your appointments and move stuff around."

"Thanks, Molly."

"No problem, Aydin. See you soon."

Knock! Knock!

"Yeah." I grabbed a case file from the drawer, turning when the door pushed open with Amelia dressed in a crisp white shirt and thigh-high jeans.

"I never got a chance to say thank you."

"For what?"

"Not casting me aside without a safety net."

She looked around the room and noticed my medals from the navy.

"You're welcome."

"Do you miss it?"

"What?"

"The navy, the brotherhood."

"Sometimes, but I have most of my guys with me that made it out."

"Your mom's really sweet."

"She likes you."

"Really!" Amelia leaned on the edge of my desk.

"Not sure what spell you put on her, but she likes you, and Josiah's already tried to claim you."

"Josiah's a sweetheart."

I made an annoyed sigh. Josiah wouldn't know what to do with a woman like her.

"He's not your type."

"How do you know?"

Amelia grabbed the family photo off my desk.

"I just do."

"What type of woman are you into?"

She gazed over at me.

"Women who can hold their own, speak their mind, but soft when my tongue is sending them into realms of pleasure they've never known." I watched as her lips parted at my statement.

"Surprised."

"Surprised by what?"

I took the photo out of her hand.

"The moment I spoke my mind, you fired me."

At her statement, I watched the smirk dance across her face. I licked my lips and leaned in close, not sure if what I was doing made sense in my mind, or if we'd end this weird attraction before it started.

Amelia raised her hand and caressed my cheek.

"You're a distraction."

"You told me that excuse."

"Then believe it."

"Only if you kiss me." She moved in so close, and I could tell her breathing rose in excitement.

Not one to be challenged, I cupped her chin and pecked her lips. She moaned, and my dick stood at attention. I used both hands and hovered over her mouth, sucking on her lips before slowly easing my tongue to open her.

"Mhmmmmm…." I groaned, deepening the kiss. I felt the goose bumps rise on her skin.

"I see your protection comes with perks." Molly cleared her throat, and we pulled away. Amelia jumped off my desk in embarrassment. Nasir and Nicco grinned and stood behind her.

"Molly! You're back." Amelia ran and hugged her.

"Just in time to catch the show," she teased.

Amelia looked from me to Molly.

"We were just talking," Amelia said.

"Never talked to Molly like that," Nicco joked, and Molly smacked him in the stomach.

"Shut up, Nicco," Molly argued.

"Can you ladies excuse us for a moment?"

"I'll be in my room." Amelia walked out with Molly.

* * *

AMELIA TRIED to distance herself after Molly, Nasir, and Nicco left a few hours ago. It was going on five in the afternoon, and we'd covered enough ground to have the airports, trains, and most of the police aware of what Addison and her team were up to. I stepped out of my bedroom after changing clothes and knocked on her door. I didn't hear an answer, so I pushed forward and saw she wasn't inside, but the shower was on. I started to leave to give her privacy.

"Hey, did you need something?"

I froze, completely speechless at how beautiful she looked and bit my bottom lip.

"Wanted to see if you were hungry."

"I could eat."

"Get dressed, and I'll meet you out front."

"Where are we going?"

"What do you have a taste for?"

"Gumbo." Amelia walked to the closet and pulled out a black jumpsuit.

"Okay, I'll look it up once you get ready."

"Great, I won't be long."

"Cool."

"Is something wrong?"

"No, why'd you say that?"

"You look like you want to say something."

"Uh… no. Let me get out of your way."

An hour and the half later, I pulled the chair out for Amelia and took the seat across from her at Belle's Seafood Restaurant. She told me it was the best place that sold gumbo in Tennessee.

"Thanks for taking me out."

"Not a problem. I knew being stuck under me for too long would drive you crazy." I chuckled. She agreed and nodded.

"Hello, I'm Stevie. I'll be your waitress. Would you like something to drink?"

Our waitress placed our menus down, and I motioned for Amelia to go first.

"Let's see. What do I have a taste for?" She lifted her finger to tap on her jaw in thought.

"Can I get a ginger ale, and I'm ready to order."

"Sure, and for you, sir?" Stevie asked.

"Same thing." Even though I came with extra backup

protection, Nicco and Nasir sat two tables away, and we had guards outside the restaurant. I needed to have a clear mind if something shifted.

"Sounds good. What would you like to eat?"

"I'll take the Cajun gumbo with shrimp please." Amelia passed her menu over, and I did the same.

"I'll have your food brought out shortly." Stevie smiled, angled to the next table, and took their orders before going to the kitchen.

"Any leads on Addison?" Amelia wrapped her pink lips around the straw in the water, I shifted in my seat to get comfortable.

"A few, but nothing panned out."

"My life is completely a mess."

"It won't be for long. You can't let her win."

"Can I ask you a personal question?"

"Yeah."

"Have you slept with Addison?"

I choked on my drink, spilling it on my shirt.

"Who told you that?"

"She basically said you belong to her."

I know my face held a hard grimace. Addison's manipulative and thought because she came from money, she could have anything she wanted. It was probably the first time ever that a man stood up to her and denied her advances. Honestly, she's a beautiful woman. For me, it takes more than beauty to grab my attention, which was why the second Amelia spoke, it sparked my curiosity to keep her talking. I was a jerk the night I first ran into her. Since she worked alongside me, we'd gotten to know each other, and her laugh was something I looked forward to hearing every day.

"Addison's delusional, and I've never slept with her."

"Have you wanted to sleep with her?"

"No. Look at me, Amelia." I reached over and palmed her hand.

"What if someone sees?"

"See's what?"

"Us holding hands."

"I don't care about that."

"You're my boss."

"I can fire you."

We both broke out into laughter.

"First time I've heard you laugh."

Stevie came to the table with our food, interrupting Amelia before she could finish.

"Cajun gumbo with shrimp and both drinks."

"Thank you," Amelia told her.

"You two enjoy and let me know if you need anything."

"I'm starving." Amelia lifted her napkin and placed it on her lap.

"Me too." She caught my stare and might have thought I was talking about the food, but the remembrance of her kiss lingered in my mind.

AMELIA

Two weeks later.

After dinner, Aydin and I got along great and had a routine down where we would go in the office together and back home, then hang out with the guys and Dani on the weekend. I thought at first he would get tired of me being in his space so much, but I was wrong. I learned so much about him and vice versa with me. Today, we were going to my parents' house for dinner, but right now, we stopped at the grocery store to pick up a few items. One thing I kept from him was my plans for after the Addison situation was resolved. After a talk with Molly, and her encouragement, I wanted to branch out on my own with a business that offered operations management for other businesses. I'd have a small staff to start out and put people in place at companies to keep the work simple for other businesses.

"Do you want steak or chicken?" We stopped at the frozen food aisle, and it was funny to have three big burly guys surround me at the store. The compromise for me to still do my normal routine was met with Nicco and Reggie, with Aydin right by my side.

"Whatever you want."

"How about both?"

"Sure."

"This is your house, Aydin. You have to give your input."

Ever since we kissed, it wasn't talked about again, but the tension was there. The desire between my thighs every night when we went to bed in opposite directions caused me to bring out my little pink toy at night. I tried to be quiet as much as possible, but I knew he heard me a time or two. The grumpiness came out the other day when I asked Nicco if he wanted coffee for breakfast. He said as long as it was creamy and sweet. The look in Aydin's eyes was one of a man ready to kill, and the joke was innocent.

"Both, Amelia." He pushed the cart forward, and I grabbed both packages and tossed them in the cart.

"See, all you have to do is give in to me the first time, and we wouldn't have these problems."

"You think so."

"Nicco, what do you think?"

"I'm out of this conversation." Nicco held his hands up in mock surrender.

"Why?" I pouted, poking my lip out.

"Because Aydin will kill me if I answer wrong."

I saw Aydin's left eye twitch, and I giggled.

"Ignore him, Nicco. I'm the boss."

"He knows, and that's the problem," Nicco joked, and I slapped hands with him. Aydin pushed the cart forward and ignored us. I ran to catch up and lock my arm around his. He looked over at me and winked.

"You're too easy," I said.

"Coming from you, the spoiled brat."

"You made me this way." I stuck my tongue out.

"That tongue is going to get you in trouble."

"Says who?"

"Me." He leaned and kissed me on the top of my head.

"We need vegetables and some fruit for my morning smoothie."

He stopped at the veggie aisle.

After we packed our cart and headed to the register, I tried to pay with my card, and Aydin pushed my hand to the side.

"What are you doing?"

"You're not paying."

"Aydin, I live rent free in your home. I have to pull my weight."

"You do when you cook and do your job at the office."

"But I could do more."

"That's enough, I'm paying." He handed the cashier his card, and they bagged the groceries and loaded up the car. He opened my door and walked around to hop in the driver's seat.

"My parents just texted me and said to bring wine."

He started the car, turned, and drove back in the opposite direction to the liquor store. Reggie and Nicco followed in another SUV, and I sat back to let the silence clear my head. Not sure if the right time was now or if I should wait, but I knew secrets weren't good to be kept between us.

"I need to tell you something."

"What's wrong?"

He pulled up to the red light.

"My work with the company has inspired me to try to do something on my own."

His brows hiked in confusion.

"What does that mean?"

"When I quit—"

"What do you mean quit? You've been there less than six months."

"I understand, and I love my job, but I want to have my own business."

"What type of business?"

"The same thing but on a bigger scale."

He pulled in front of the liquor store, shut the car off, and sighed.

"You just now decided to tell me this."

"Aydin."

"We have your parents' dinner. This can wait." He climbed out of the car, shut the door, and headed in with Nicco behind him. Reggie stood next to the car to keep me company.

* * *

THE DOOR OPENED, and my parents stood together. I stepped in close to give them a hug first and introduced Aydin. I offered for Nicco and Reggie to have dinner with us, but they declined to stay on alert. It was awkward after the conversation in the car.

"Aydin, these are my parents Cassandra and Conrad." Dad stuck his hand out, and Aydin came up behind me and extended his hand.

"Nice to meet you, Mr. and Mrs. Edwards."

"You too, Aydin. Come in and have a seat," Mom responded.

"Our daughter told us you work together." Dad shut the door, and we sat on the couch.

Aydin handed the bottle of wine to my mom.

"I hired her as my operations manager of my security firm."

"Security." Dad paused.

"Navy."

"I remember my time in the army." Dad recalled his younger years.

My dad talked with me only a little about his time when he was overseas, but once he was finished in the army, he went to college and married my mom. Then I came along.

"Amelia, come with me in the kitchen. The food is almost ready."

I followed her and took the small bowls out of her hands.

"He's cute."

"Mom."

She leaned against the counter, planting her hand on her hip.

"You like him."

I lowered my head to avoid her.

"We kissed," I mumbled.

"He's your boss."

"I know."

"We didn't raise you to be someone's little plaything."

I took the bowls to the table and spread them out for the salad.

"Aydin's different. Early on, he fired me."

"Fired you?"

"A long story, but we're in a good place now."

Mom placed the wine glasses on the table.

"I have to tell you something, and I don't want you to freak out."

"Tell me and let me decide how I want to react."

"I live with him."

"Live with who?"

"Aydin."

"Why?"

"I found something out, and people tried to kill me."

"Kill you!" she shrieked, and I put my hand up to hush her before my dad got involved.

"Kill who?" Dad ran into the kitchen, looked from me to Mom. I rubbed my forehead from the migraine that formed.

"Nothing, Dad."

"Who's trying to kill our child?" Mom marched toward Aydin.

The simple dinner I expected to have completely changed the mood of the night.

"Mrs. Edwards." Aydin tried to calm the situation.

"No, we need to call the police."

"The police are on the case. My brother works for the police," Aydin stated.

"You're staying with us." Mom pointed at me.

"Ma, I'm safe. I promise."

"Is someone going to tell me what's going on?" Dad demanded.

"I live with Aydin under his protection because somebody tried to kill us," I blurted out.

Dad took a seat at the table, rubbing a hand down his face.

"Is she safe with you?" Dad spoke to Aydin.

"Yes, sir."

"She's our world," Dad told him.

"Amelia, I'm not happy about this." Mom sat next to Dad.

"Aydin can tell you from the beginning, I wasn't happy." Aydin came around to sit next to me and rubbed my leg under the table.

"All right, the second a piece of hair is out of place on her head…" Dad threatened.

Aydin raised his hand in understanding.

"Daddy, I'm fine. I trust Aydin."

* * *

A WEEK LATER, Dani, Molly, and I sat around Aydin's house and drank margaritas outside. I invited them over to hang out with me for the weekend. Even Rebecca and my mom were included, but both women had plans already and couldn't make it today. Honestly, I was happy because I could be free in my conversation about Aydin.

"So, your dad threatened Aydin." Molly picked up her drink.

"I was so embarrassed."

"What did Aydin say about being threatened by Conrad?"

"He understood, and they went off to drink whiskey together and talk."

"Any new updates?" Molly wondered.

"He's kept it from me for the most part. The second I told him about me opening my business, our conversations changed."

"He's used to having you around," Dani said.

Dani was correct. I enjoyed being around him, but I did miss my apartment and going out with friends. My life was different from when I bumped into him in need of a job. From my time working at TN, I had money saved so I could go out on my own.

"I do miss my apartment but have grown to like waking up in his place."

"In his place and bed." Dani smirked, pretending to kiss her hand.

Molly bit into her taco.

"Have you two taken the next step?"

"No, we kissed."

"He's sexy," Dani said.

I scoffed and ate some of my nachos.

"What are you afraid would happen if you slept with him?"

"He's never made a move beyond the kiss."

"Then you need to take the first step. You don't need to wait for the man," Molly encouraged me, and I looked out in the yard, realizing he'd played it safe with me, thinking I was some soft, untouchable doll.

"First step," I muttered.

AYDIN

A day later.

The chill of the rain poured down outside, and I watched her body fall across the bed when the lights turned out. I didn't regret having her stay here with me while I figured out who was behind trying to kill her. Nasir thought it was a bad idea, that I would lose focus on what the mission was, but the way she'd felt in my arms when she ran from those bullets that night, I felt it was only right. We'd become closer, and tonight would take us to another level.. I didn't know how to explain it to myself, let alone when Nasir pushed it in my head that I was falling for her beyond our work relationship. After I watched her remove her wet clothes, her eyes dropped as I gazed at her sexy frame against my sheets.

"Never shy away from me."

Her skin grew hot, and her eyes widened. Her cheeks blushed when she ran a hand up her chest and squeezed her breasts. I went to place the candles down on the dresser and stripped my clothes off. Amelia ran her tongue across her bottom lip, and I heard a low rumble in her voice.

"What did you say?" My heart drummed against my ribs.

"I said I hope I can please you." She clutched the sheets.

The desire in her eyes showed me Amelia was more submissive than I realized. Tonight, I planned on making her mine. I cupped her chin and watched as her breathing spiked. She reached up to plant her hand on my cheek. We peered into each other's eyes, and the weakness I wanted to avoid became harder to uphold. She leaned up and pressed her lips to mine, causing me to bend down further and hover over her body with her left leg cocked open and right leg flat on the bed. I gripped the sheets, as my tongue snaked in and captured hers. The sound of her moan caused my heart to flutter. Her arms gripped both sides of my back, pulling back to hear her whimper.

"Aydin..." she cooed and touched my belly. I shivered underneath.

"You're a bad habit, Amelia." The voice I didn't recognize was a low growl. I caressed her cheek. She smiled and gripped my shaft.

"Habits can't be good or bad."

Her statement caused my left brow to rise.

"How so?"

The rain pellets fell against the window, and goose bumps formed on her arms.

"I made a choice to be here, and you did as well. It doesn't matter what the outcome will be. I'm a big girl, Aydin." Her leg wrapped around my waist, and she lined my dick up to her pussy. Slowly, I sank deeper into her walls without any plans to come up for air.

"Shit!" Her body inclined toward mine.

Her head fell back, and she arched her chest forward

when I rocked in and out slowly. I reached to grab her right leg, angled it wider, and continued my strokes. Amelia went to pull me closer, and I refused, licking my thumb and flicking her clit. The tightness in my chest grew, and I felt something I couldn't explain to her or myself. I wanted morning, noon, and night.

"Aydin! Right there," she whined and moved her hand up to her breasts. I leaned over and flicked my tongue around her sweet nipple, licking around her brown areola. All this time, I tortured myself by keeping her at a distance and missed out on her sweet, warm, perfect body.

"I need more," I growled, abruptly pulling out. I dropped face down to eat her until she screamed my name.

"Ooohhh…" she cooed. Her hand went to the back of my head, pushing me further in between her warm pussy. I slid my tongue inside, closed my eyes, and sucked on her nub as if it was my favorite breakfast. She gasped.

"Shit, MeMe." I didn't know where that nickname came from, but she was like my favorite dessert that I could eat every day for the rest of my life.

Amelia closed her legs around my head and convulsed at the work I put into her pleasure.

I smirked and captured all her juices that trickled down her thighs, trailing kisses up her legs and stomach. I swirled my tongue in her navel and swiped it up to her left breast, gripping it in my hand like a newborn child.

"MeMe, you're dangerous." After pulling away from her left breast, I focused on the right one. Our lips met, and our hands interlocked. Then, we became one again.

"I want to feel you forever," she whispered, and I pushed forward, pounding in powerful thrusts. Her cries kept me in a state of some drug I didn't want to come down from. Not once did I stop, and my hands gripped her hips. Sweat dripped down my chest to my stomach, and I felt her clench around my dick.

"Are you ready to come for me, baby?"

"Yasss!" she screamed. Her eyes fluttered with mist. "Yes, Aydin! Oh my God." Her entire body tensed.

Her breath hitched, and she soon came down from her orgasm. My dick was still hard when I stroked a few seconds longer. I pulled the condom off and released in my hand.

"Now for seconds." Amelia climbed over me and ran her nails down my chest.

"This was about you tonight." Amelia brushed her lips against my mouth, then sat up, wrapping herself in a blanket. Even though it poured down and the lights went out, the heat in the bedroom caused sparks to fly. Her hand rested on my arm and her leg bent across my thigh, as she bounced up and down.

"You're amazing," she said in awe.

I sucked in a breath when she bent down and held her breasts up to my lip.

"God, you're beautiful," I moaned and appraised her body all night long.

"Never take your hands off me." Amelia kissed my forehead and drew me in close.

* * *

THE NEXT MORNING, I woke up to an empty bed. Remembering our night together, I smiled. I flipped the covers off me and headed to the bathroom. I found my pants, headed to the kitchen, and found Amelia at the stove, dancing to music as she flipped pancakes. I walked up behind her and wrapped my arms around her waist, pulling her back to my chest to kiss the left side of her neck.

"Morning."

"Morning, baby."

"Are you hungry?" She angled her head to look up at me, and I pecked her on the lips.

"Not for food." I slid a hand under her shirt and noticed she didn't wear panties. I moved my hand up and grasped her left breast.

"Last night was amazing," she moaned, dropping the pancake on the plate. I sucked on her neck, slid down her stomach and slowly slid a finger in her pussy.

"Shit!" she gasped, slamming her hand on the counter.

"Come back to bed," I demanded.

"Aydin..." she purred, and her cries of pleasure motivated me to turn her around and pick her up on top of the counter.

"I woke up alone."

"You were finally sleeping without watching me."

"What are you talking about?"

"I know you stay up sometimes to watch me sleep."

I stepped between her legs.

"We need to get to the office."

I peppered kisses across her shoulder.

"Work can wait."

"Nope." Amelia nudged me back and jumped off the counter.

Amelia grabbed the plate of pancakes, sausage, and fruit and handed me the bread to sit down and eat breakfast together. Two hours later, we arrived at the office and parked.

"Are we having lunch together?"

"I have a meeting with the bank," she said.

She walked ahead of me in the door, and I reached for her hand.

"Nicco and Reggie will drive you."

"Hey, are you cool with this?"

"Am I happy about you working somewhere else, no. But I'm proud of you."

I walked her to her office. She opened the door, and a bouquet of flowers sat on the desk.

"You didn't have to do this." Amelia looked over her shoulder at me.

"I didn't."

She picked up the card to read it.

"He can't save you," she read aloud.

"Let me see." I took the card out of her hands and read over the words. I recognized the handwriting as belonging to Addison.

"She's still out there." Amelia walked into my chest.

"Aye, she can't hurt you. I promise."

"How did she get to my office?"

"Good question." I lifted the phone and dialed Molly.

"Hey, girl," Molly cheerfully answered.

"It's me."

"Aydin, why are you calling from Amelia's phone?"

"When did you get to the office today?"

"Usual time, around eight."

"I need the company log of who delivered the flowers."

I heard her typing on the computer.

"Let me check."

"Addison was here."

"Here as in the office," Molly replied.

"Yeah, Amelia's pretty upset."

"It shows that the flowers were signed off by Carly, but that doesn't mean anything."

"True, let me check the cameras." I hung up and rubbed Amelia's back as she cried softly in my arms.

"My parents."

"Shushhh… Your parents are fine. Come with me to my office."

"But."

"We'll get through this together." I pressed a kiss on her forehead.

* * *

MOLLY HELPED Amelia reshuffle some of my appointments after the flower situation earlier, and now sitting in my office, I watched the playback of the camera footage from the delivery truck. Surprised to see the man Amelia described with the scar and tattoo drove the truck and walked into my building like normal. He smiled at Carly, and she took the flowers and walked off while he deliberately looked up at the camera and smiled. That only told me that Addison explained what we did and how our business was set up. Nasir shut the door behind me and took a seat in front of my desk.

"I talked to Carly, and she doesn't remember much about the truck."

"Did they run the plates from the outside camera?"

"Yeah, and it's reported stolen by the flower company."

"He's the guy that Amelia bumped into that night."

"So, he's working with Addison."

"I put my money on it that she has all of them on her payroll."

"For him to get this close."

"Pisses me off."

"Where's Amelia?"

"With Molly in her office."

"Don't go off and do anything crazy."

"I can't promise."

"Any updates on Tristan's whereabouts?"

"He's skipped out on his apartment, and the landlord hasn't received any rent for the past two months."

"Fuck!"

"They're testing us."

"Addison thinks she's in control. I'll let her believe that but only for so long."

I reached in my pocket and removed my cell phone and dialed a number I hadn't used in a few weeks.

"Senator Edgar's office.

"Tell Senator Edgar it's Aydin Reeve."

"I'm sorry but he's out of the state at the moment."

"Where?"

"I can't give that information out, sir."

I slammed the phone down on the desk.

"He's gone."

"Out of state."

"Retrace our steps."

"Addison could be anywhere by now."

"Or the least obvious place."

"Her father's home."

Nasir and I rose at the same time and left without a word to anyone. I texted Nicco and Reggie to stay with Amelia until I got back. Thirty minutes later, we pulled up to the home of Senator Edgar and waited for the gate to open. A car left, and we jogged through the gate and up to the house. Nasir closed the door behind me, and we headed toward his office when we heard voices.

"Mr. Edgar will be gone for a few days, so make sure the house is scrubbed top to bottom," the house manager informed the housekeeper. We stood on the side of the wall, away from the living room, and waited for them to leave before going to the office.

"Yes, ma'am, Mrs. Eloise."

Eloise directed her staff to the dining area. We slipped down the hall into his office, then closed the door.

"Check the cabinets, and I'll look in his computer." I sat at his desk.

"He'd be stupid to be involved," Nasir commented.

"Addison was stupid and see where we are."

I checked the bottom desk drawer and noticed stacks of papers. I flipped through but nothing stood out beyond speeches. Checking on the right side, I pulled it open and found the same sheets and a calendar of his events. Aggravated at the lack of evidence, I moved to the top drawer in front of me and pulled it open. I saw messages and returned calls he needed to make. One piece of paper had a few numbers on top, and I took a picture with my phone.

"Nothing over here so far."

"Keep looking. Has to be here somewhere." I turned to his computer and logged in with no password lock.

"Mostly bills he sponsored."

"No password on his computer."

"That never happens, especially with a senator."

"False computer."

"You think?"

I peered around his room and noticed pictures on his wall, plaques from awards, and a bar area in the corner. I squinted my eyes and noticed behind the bar a small black safe.

"Look at that." I rose out of the seat and went to the bar, moved it to the side, and squatted down to look at the lock.

"Interesting."

"The combination." I tried to think of what the code could be.

AYDIN

Nasir drove back to the office, and I sat in the car and flipped through the documents we pulled from Edgar's safe, wondering how long he'd been embezzling. The picture I took of the numbers from his desk opened the safe, and I grabbed everything I could take before Eloise or the housekeeper would notice anything moved.

"Are you going to confront him?"

"I want to play this the right way."

"If he's behind the embezzlement, he knows Addison is doing some crooked shit," Nasir spat.

"The SEC would love what we found."

"Private planes, cars, and trips aren't on a senator's salary alone."

"See if you can pull his flights for the last few months. Maybe Addison joined him."

Nasir parked back at the office, and we climbed out.

"Carly can look into the numbers and offshore accounts."

"Call a meeting."

I passed the documents to Nasir and went to find Amelia. I saw the door of her office crack open and heard laughter. Stepping inside, I lightly knocked on the door.

"Hey," she said.

"You eat?" I walked around her desk, bent down, and kissed her on the lips.

"Yep. Molly ordered us barbecue sandwiches from Tops."

"Where did you and Nasir go?" Molly questioned.

"A lead." I kept it vague, as not to worry them.

"You found out who sent the flowers?"

I palmed her hand.

"The guy you accidentally bumped into the night of the party was the same man.."

"Wait. You mean it wasn't an accident when we met," Amelia clarified.

"For now, it looks like he works with Addison."

"We'll never be rid of her."

"Yes, you will."

"Aydin, I shouldn't have brought my problems your way."

"You didn't."

"But I did," she whined.

"Amelia, even if you didn't overhear, someone else might have," Molly told me, and I agreed.

"Just crazy to me how she's stayed one step ahead." Amelia reached to grab my hand.

"Edgar's gotten his hands dirty."

"The senator." Amelia's shocked expression covered her face.

"At the moment, I can't say he's working with his daughter, but we know he's not innocent at all."

"Maybe time to pull in the FBI, Aydin."

"I will, but not yet. To go up against him, I need to verify each document."

Amelia looked off.

"Amelia."

"Huh."

"Stop worrying."

"I know."

"Good, I'm here."

We both leaned into a kiss, and I promised we'd leave here in a few minutes after my meeting to get dinner. Once I walked out of her office, I went to the conference room and saw the guys sitting around the table.

Nasir filled everyone in on what we found.

"How do you want us to handle him?" Nicco asked.

As I stood at the front of the conference table, I looked around at my team and thought of the sacrifices we'd made for our country, and to have people like Edgar and Addison betray, lie, and kill people for political gain. It caused my stomach to drop in defeat.

"Put people on his house."

"No updates on her place in Chicago?" Carly said.

"Tristan is in the wind and more than likely with her." I slid my hands in my pockets.

"He's on the intelligence committee." Nicco read through the file.

"If we alert too soon, it'll backfire on us," I said.

"So we play the background," Nasir responded.

"Until they make another move."

"By the way things are going, it won't be long," Nicco called out.

"Double protection around the clock on Amelia's parents' home, my place, and my parents'."

"Did you tell Wesley?"

"I'm going to talk to him tomorrow."

"All right."

"Try to get some sleep, boss." Nicco stood, and we shook hands.

"Thanks for sticking with her."

"She's like a sister to me now."

* * *

AFTER MY MEETING, I picked up Amelia and instead of going out to eat, we ordered takeout and came straight home. I pushed the door open and reset the alarm, Reggie honked the horn, and I waved before locking the door. Amelia carried a bag of her favorite Mexican food over to the table, removed her jacket, and kicked off her shoes.

"I'm going to give you a bath."

"Come sit first."

She held her arm out for me, and I picked her up, sat, and placed her on my lap.

"You look tired."

"No more than usual."

"Are you tired of me?"

"Where did that come from?"

I rubbed a hand up and down her back.

"Sorry my life became an endless rollercoaster for you."

"Have I said that to you?"

"No, but—"

I shushed her and caressed her cheek.

"I would never grow tired of you."

"It's my fault you're in this mess."

"Your mess is my mess."

"I'm serious, Aydin." Amelia tried to stand, and I tightened my grip around her waist to keep her from moving.

"Stop running from me."

"You should be at your business, sleeping with random women, not holed up with me every second."

"I like being holed up with you."

"Still." She placed her hand on my chest.

"The only complaint I have is that I didn't meet you sooner."

"Doubt you'd have ever looked at me."

"You're wrong."

"I'm not your type; we're polar opposites."

"You bring out the best in me and, sunshine, your radiance makes me want to be better."

"Promise?"

"Always."

"Are we going to your parents' tomorrow?" She started to pull the food out of the bag.

"Yep, I need to talk to my brother. My mom wants to hang out with you again."

Amelia popped a chip in her mouth.

"I've met everyone except your dad."

"He's way more laid back than my mom."

"Funny, because your mom is more like you."

"I guess you could say that."

"So, I'm more like your dad." Amelia pointed at herself.

"Which means it's a perfect match."

"If they've lasted this long, then I could see how opposites do attract."

Once we gathered the napkins out of the bag, I sat next to her on the couch, and we ate in silence while the movie played. Two hours later, I had a hot bubble bath, wine, and her favorite candles lit, ready to relax. I sat behind her and ran a towel over her leg. I kissed the nape of her neck.

"Sleepy."

Her eyes were closed.

"That feels good."

I ran a towel across her stomach.

"The second we slept together, you haven't slept alone since," Amelia teased me.

"I like you in my bed."

"I wondered why."

I moved my hand to her right breast and pinched her nipple gently. She arched her back in my arms.

"You know why."

"Does everyone at the office know we're together?"

"Probably." I shrugged.

"Are you okay with that?"

I pinched her left nipple, and she moaned.

"My personal life is no one's business."

"I know, but I'd hate for anyone to think I got the position because I slept with the boss."

"The only one you should be concerned about is me."

I cupped her pussy, and her leg extended wider to give me more room.

"Ohhhh…" She covered my hand with hers.

"Let's go to bed."

"Kiss me."

As she guided my finger in and out, I sucked on her top lip at the same time, wanting to take her right here in the tub while my erection poked at her back. Amelia adjusted to her side, and I gripped her around the waist to sit her in my lap. We made out for the next ten minutes before the water turned cold, and I went to take a shower. I carried her out of the bathroom and placed her on the bed in nothing but a towel, admiring her soft curves and smooth skin. I trailed kisses up her arm to her lips, grabbed the comforter to cover us, and pushed between her thighs to widen the space, teasing her a few times with just the head.

"Aydin!" she whined. After the third time, Amelia slid

her hand up and down my large girth and pulled me forward.

"Fuck!" I shouted.

"I missed this." She gripped my face and kissed me softly.

"We have all night."

"Tell me again."

"I'll never leave you."

"Promise."

"Promise forever."

"Keep going."

The next day, Aydin took me to his parents' home for lunch, and I saw where Aydin got his protector nature from with his dad. All afternoon, he'd assist or remove any obstacles from his wife's hands or handle any problem she experienced, and it was something I'd thought would make a marriage work. For them to have been married so long and still playful and silly with each other was another bonus. All three boys were here, and Josiah brought a date, which surprised me and Aydin. Carly didn't seem like she'd go for the games with men like Josiah, who loved to be surrounded by women and flirted constantly.

"Carly, what do you do again?" Rebecca put the plate of mashed potatoes on the table.

"I do tech support at Aydin's firm," Carly answered.

"That's impressive." Rebecca sat next to Wesley.

"Amelia, you work there as well, correct?" Cole inquired, and I took the plate of asparagus from Aydin.

"Operations manager."

"Glad she keeps him on his toes," Rebeca chimed in on our conversation.

"I'm the lucky one." I gazed at Aydin.

"Please don't blow up my brother's head," Josiah joked, and Aydin glared.

"Shut up." Aydin placed his hand on top of mine.

"We'd love to meet your parents, Amelia."

Aydin and I hadn't talked if our relationship was serious or not to the point of meeting parents. It just happened gradually, and neither of us forced the other in a situation that we'd be uncomfortable with. To hear Rebecca request to meet my parents was surprising but sweet at the same time…

"Uhm."

"We'll arrange a big dinner one day," Aydin answered for me. He noticed my nervousness.

I leaned over to whisper in his ear, "Thank you."

"I got your back."

"What are you two doing after lunch?"

"I have an appointment at the bank."

"Is everything all right?" Rebecca asked.

"I'm in the early stages of opening my own business."

"That's wonderful."

"Thanks."

"Brains and beauty. Aydin, please don't mess this up," Rebecca stated, and we all laughed at her comment.

"Carly, how long have you and Josiah dated?" I probed, watching Josiah squirm in his seat.

"About four months now," Carly told me.

"Surprised you've been able to deal with the youngest boy. He can be a handful." Cole bit into his sandwich.

"She gave me a hard time in the beginning," Josiah stated, and Carly agreed.

"Wesley's the last one to bring a date around," Rebecca announced.

"Rather get a root canal," Wesley replied, and Rebecca smacked him on the back of the head. We laughed and continued to talk of the work they did and my future plans.

* * *

AYDIN SHUT the car door and waved at his parents. Turning into traffic, he headed out to the main road toward the bank. The loan manager needed me to come in and fill out some paperwork before he submitted it on my behalf.

"Where is your head at?"

I ran a hand across Aydin's hair and down his cheek.

"Nothing." He changed lanes and looked out his rearview mirror.

"Shouldn't take long at the bank."

"I know, but that's the last thing on my mind."

"Any word on Edgar?"

"No, but let's talk about something else."

Pop! Pop!

"Arghhh!" I screamed when the side mirror was shot off.

"Get down!"

Nicco and Reggie were still behind us. We drove into traffic, as I prayed they were okay. We were still fifteen minutes from his home and five minutes from the bank. The car swerved from left to right, tried to avoid hitting another car as much as possible.

"Aydin!" I screamed as the bullet pierced the back window. He sideswiped another car to get out of the way.

"Open the compartment and pass me the gun."

Tears fell down my cheek, as I popped it open and

grabbed his 9mm. I'd never shot a gun in my life and didn't want to have the responsibility to take someone's life.

"I need you to put your seatbelt on." Aydin picked up his phone.

"What are you about to do?"

"We're blocked by three cars, hold tight." Nicco answered the phone.

"Shit! They probably watched us from my parents' house," Aydin growled.

"Nasir is sending some men to keep an eye out."

"Thanks for looking out."

"Get off on the next exit. We'll try to box them in."

"It's one car?"

Pop! Popppp!

"A tinted-out black SUV," Nicco replied. I heard bullets over the call.

"I need to get her home safe."

"Slow a little, then speed up. Almost there."

"Hurry! Take the wheel." Aydin ended the call.

"Aydin! Oh, my God!" He lowered the window and sent bullets to the car Nicco described. I held onto the steering wheel to avoid a crash.

Pop!

Aydin pressed the gas and took a sharp turn to get on the off-ramp. I held onto the dashboard and saw Nicco come up behind us, blocking the car that was shooting. We drove through the red light, and another car honked his horn. My chest rose up and down, and my hands shook as tears pooled into my eyes.

"I'm here," Aydin comforted me.

"Yeahhh… Yeah," I stuttered, grabbing his hand.

After another five minutes of driving in circles, we pulled up to his house and hugged each other. Then the door opened, and he pointed the gun, about to shoot.

"Wooo… It's me." Nicco held his hands up.

"Get her inside." Aydin jumped out of his car. Reggie stood with Aydin and watched as traffic went up and down the street.

"Do you think they followed us?" I probed.

"We hit their tire, and it flipped over."

I raised a hand to my mouth in shock.

"How much more damage can she do?" I looked out the window.

"Aydin's going to be fine. Try to stay away from the windows."

"Nervous they'll hurt him."

"Aydin's tough."

"Not from bullets."

"We're trained for battle."

"Is that supposed to make me feel better?"

"Does it?"

"Not really."

"Aydin's the best in the business, and he cares about you."

"Thanks, Nicco."

"Try to relax."

"You're right."

Nicco left the house, and I lifted the phone and dialed Dani's number.

"Mrs. Edwards or should I call you Mrs. Reeve," Dani suggested.

"Glad someone can laugh."

"What happened?"

"Girl, I was just in a shoot-out."

"Shoot-out!" Dani screamed. I removed the phone from my ear.

"I'm fine, Dani."

"Do you need me to come over?"

"No, the less people I have to worry about the better."

"Amelia, what the hell are you talking about? I'm your best friend," she barked.

The door opened, and Aydin, Nicco, and Nasir stepped in and shut the door.

"Aydin just came into the house."

"Are you hurt?"

"No, we made it back to his house."

Our eyes connected, and I knew he felt guilty.

"For now, I'll leave it alone. But you better keep me updated."

"Promise, I'll call you." She ended the call, and Aydin stood against the door of the hallway.

"Where's Reggie?"

"I sent him home and switched him with two more guys," Aydin responded.

"Was he hit?" I jumped up and stood in front of him.

"He's fine. We change shifts often," Nasir spoke.

"Are you two hungry? We have leftovers," I suggested, heading to the kitchen.

"Before we hit the road, we can eat."

We still had lasagna, baked potato, and chicken leftover because I liked to overcook even when I was home. I moved around in the kitchen, still a little shaken up from what happened and prayed Addison was caught soon. I felt a pair of strong hands around me and released a long-held breath. I turned the oven on and unwrapped the chicken, two potatoes, and a pan of lasagna before I slid them in the oven.

"Talk to me."

"I'm worried about you."

"I'll be fine."

"Glad you were with me this time."

I turned around to face him.

"I apologize for letting them get so close to you."

"You have nothing to apologize for."

"It's my job to protect you."

"And you have." I stood on my tippy toes and reached an arm around his neck, fixated on his lips.

"She's going to pay."

"Long as you don't get hurt."

"My job is dangerous, baby."

"That's what scares me."

"She'll show her face, but there's something I need to tell you."

"What?"

"You can't go back to your place again."

I paused to look in his eyes, pushing back out of his hold.

"So, I'm a prisoner forever."

"No, just a little longer until we can grab Tristan or this guy that bumped into you."

"Addison's not about to control my life, Aydin."

"Only temporarily."

"All right."

"Thank you."

Aydin squeezed my ass and pulled me in close. We engaged in a long kiss before a voice was cleared.

"Sorry. Let me get dinner started." I glanced from Aydin to Nicco.

The next afternoon.

I slipped my dress over my body and watched his eyes narrow in praise and want. He'd done what he said he would and kept me protected. Aydin sat on the couch with both hands behind his back, licking his lips. As I drew closer, I bent down and kissed him on the lips. He leveled with a look that I'd better prepare to not try to run when he got started. He lifted his arms around my back and pressed me close to his chest.

"How is your day?" I pulled back and waited for an answer. I ran a hand through his hair.

"Long, we have to fly to Chicago." He cradled my jaw and gazed at me.

"Did you talk to Senator Edgar?" Aydin watched me intently when I lifted up. I reached down, unbuckled his pants, and took control of his dick that sprang up ready for me. His tongue sought out my mouth and forced entry. He moaned in pleasure.

"We can talk about that later." He grunted when I jerked him off and got on my knees to take him in my mouth.

Nasir told me earlier about how Aydin was acting at the office and was pissed off that no one could find Tristan or Addison. For so long, he'd been the premier agency to capture criminals and somehow, Addison and her money had caused more problems. Aydin hissed and tried to grip the back of my head to control my movements. I pushed him away and trailed the kiss over his mushroom head and down to his balls.

"Wait, baby."

Ignoring him, I stroked up from the tip to the base and sucked him in completely. Then his eyes closed, and I looked at him in bliss. Aydin gripped the pillow next to him, and I grinned, bobbing my head up and down, then forcing a loud pop.

"Come up here," he growled, tossing the pillows off the couch. I was desperate for his touch.

"You know how sexy you look." He slid his arms around my back and buried his face in my chest.

"Tell me."

"I want you all the time, baby."

I grinned and slid up and down. Our rhythm matched, and I felt my legs tremble. He moved his hands down to my thighs. I sat back with my hands behind me and rode him while he gazed into my eyes.

Whap!

Aydin smacked me on the ass, stood with us still joined together, and laid me on the back of the couch. He slammed into me and pressed his lips to mine. Sucking on my tongue, I gasped in euphoria of his warm, strong arms around me.

"Fuck, Amelia," he groaned and sank his fingers in my skin. My head spun around in a cosmic light and I met his strokes.

"I... Arghhh." I felt the same heat and dizziness as

before and knew he brought me another high. Then our combined juices trailed onto the couch. He thrusted with precision and gave me what I wanted. It was like he knew I was right on the edge and before I went over the cliff, he pulled back, and my heart felt overwhelmed with joy.

"Faster." I bit into his shoulder, and my nails stung his back.

"I'll always protect you." He promised with his words and body once again. I wrapped my arms around his neck and drew him in close while we laid together in bliss from our lovemaking.

* * *

ADDISON BECAME BOLDER with her attacks, still refusing to back down after this second shoot-out. I was ready to do anything to get peace and quiet back in my life. Like right now, I came to the Peabody Hotel to get more information on the guests that night and follow up if the man that I bumped into was with anyone else besides Addison. I put on my best smile and waited for the desk clerk to finish checking. My guards stood a few feet away, and at first, they were hesitant to bring me, but I promised I'd be in and out quickly.

"Hello. Welcome to Peabody Hotel, I'm Stephanie."

"Hi, I'm sorry to disturb you, but my boss forced me to come and ask." I thought of a lie that would get me access.

"Hopefully, I can help."

"I do hope so. When you have your job on the line, you get desperate." I put on an act and wiped the fake tear that I pretended would fall.

"Tell me what I can help you with?" Stephanie pushed the box of tissues in front of me. I grabbed it and folded one in my hand.

"I was here a few weeks ago, maybe months, for Senator Edgar's daughter."

"Oh, we love Senator Edgar here."

She smiled, and I returned in kind, piling on how much I loved my job as his assistant.

"I'll be sure to tell him you've been a big help."

"What can we do for you?"

"Well, I need to see the video footage of that night and the guest list."

She shifted her eyes from behind me to her computer.

"Unfortunately, that's something I can't allow."

"I completely understand, but you'd be doing me a huge favor."

Stephanie typed on her computer.

"He wanted to get thank you notes sent out to everyone on behalf of his daughter."

"Mmmmm…"

"Is something wrong?"

"Between you and me, Addison's not liked very much at this hotel. She's always rude to the staff." Stephanie leaned back from the counter.

"That's not the first time I've heard that about her and probably won't be the last."

Stephanie pulled up a file of the guest list. I didn't want to go in the office and grab a copy when it was blocked for security reasons. He'd know I was doing more digging.

"Please don't tell anyone you got this from me." Stephanie hit print, and the documents came up on the printer. She grabbed the two-page copy and placed it on top of the counter.

"Follow me, and I'll show you the footage."

"Thank you so much, Stephanie."

Another clerk came up to the counter, and Stephanie motioned for me to follow. We headed to the employee office and sat at her desk. Stephanie set up the footage on her computer.

"Do you have a specific time?"

"I do, and you don't have to wait with me. I'd rather you not get in trouble."

Stephanie raised her wrist and checked the time on her watch.

"I'll give you five minutes, and I'll be back."

"Thank you again. You won't regret this."

"Sure. Anytime it involves Addison, I feel bad for the other person."

How would I tell her that Addison was more involved and controlling behind the Chatsworth family business? Stephanie left, and I sat in the chair to pull up four different camera angles, fast-forwarding to the times I saw Edgar or Addison in talks with a person or two. Most of the night, Addison put on a fake smile and greeted guests at the door. Out of the corner of my eye, I saw Tristan and the guy I bumped into make eye contact. Mostly, Addison steered clear of him. Edgar seemed oblivious throughout the entire night while he mixed and mingled with the guests. The moment I saw Aydin and I walk to the back, Addison scanned, then snatched out of another man's hold, and went to follow us.

"Stephanie, we need to go over the quarterly reports." I heard from the other side of the door. I didn't have time to copy the footage but emailed myself a screenshot of the gentleman right after I walked away from him. There I noticed he went into the room Addison and Tristan were in and didn't leave for a while. The door opened in the office, I cleared the screen, and jumped up to leave.

"Who are you?" an older woman with glasses and short, brown hair asked. Her badge was labeled manager, and I knew it was time to go.

"Stephanie, thank you so much for letting me apply for a job."

Stephanie stood to the side nervously. I held my hand out, and she took it as she caught on to my excuse.

"You're welcome, and our manager will be in touch if your resume checks out," Stephanie explained.

"Thank you, and it was nice meeting you both."

"You as well," Joyce replied.

I wiped the sweat beads on my brow and jogged out of the office, back toward the car when my cell rang. I looked down and saw Molly's name scrolled across.

"Hey, what are you doing later today?"

"Um, nothing much," I nervously replied. Looking out the window, I made eye contact with my driver.

"Why do you sound so nervous?"

"No reason and no plans. What do you have in mind?"

"Maybe grab some drinks with me and Dani."

"That sounds good."

"Perfect. Give me another hour, and I'll text you the place."

"Okay, I'll head home and change."

We talked a few more seconds and then hung up.

An hour and a half later, I arrived at the bar Dani took me to for the blind date. The place was crowded, with mostly couples. I took a seat next to Molly, around the three-seat table.

"You changed?" Dani pushed the dirty martini closer to me.

Lifting the drink to my lips, I nodded.

"I ran some errands today and felt like I needed to refresh before going out."

"Where's your bodyguard?"

I pointed to two tables over.

"Aydin's not taking any chances," Dani said.

"I know, and I feel guilty that his life has changed because of me."

"You didn't ask for this to happen, Amelia." Molly placed her hand on my shoulder.

Too many people in my life are affected by my choices.

"Tonight, no dark talk. We invited you out to have fun," Dani encouraged me, and I appreciated my friend for always having my back.

"How is married life, Molly? We never had a chance to catch up on the wedding."

Molly held her hand out to show her ring. I admired it the first time when she arrived back at the office.

"Wonderful. I hope you and Aydin get to experience a life that is all-consuming love."

Dani raised her glass in the air.

"Here's to all-consuming love." Dani clinked her glass with ours.

"How's work for you, Dani?" I'd been so wrapped in my life, that Dani and I didn't get much time to talk like we used to do.

"Work is work for the most part."

"Are you still dating?"

"I am, and you won't believe it, but your old blind date has found a new love."

"Really?"

A part of me was happy for him, but another part was resentful because he wasn't comfortable with my job and being around so many men. To me, everyone felt like big brothers and no amount of money would make me see them in a sexual way. Well, Aydin was a different man altogether. The presence that he exuded was intimidating and demanding, but he was sweet in how he cared for the people he loved. I continued to listen to Molly describe her wedding details. Almost everyone from the team went to her wedding. Her parents loved her husband, and the feeling was mutual from his family. The laughs we had went on for about another two hours and four drinks. I ended with water on the ride home to sober up. When I entered the bedroom and kicked my shoes off, Aydin was sleeping in bed. I'd already texted I was on my way home and not to stay up. After removing my jacket, I slipped out of the leather pants, heels, and sleeveless top and crawled in next to him. He felt me get under the covers, kissed the side of my neck, and went back to sleep. My heart felt content and happy to have him in my corner.

AMELIA

Today, I was back at my apartment to grab a few more of my things before I returned to Aydin's place. Even though he made me promise to use his guards, I refused to live like some helpless person, so they were outside in the car waiting for me. Addison was missing in the wind after Aydin confronted her in Chicago, and Tristan was fired, but charges were still pending on him for the accounting fraud. I unlocked my door and pushed forward, picking up the mail off the floor. I sighed and dropped the bills in my purse, closed the door, and turned to head to the kitchen when a glove-covered hand went over my mouth.

"Keep quiet, and I won't kill you," he harshly whispered in my ear.

I remembered the musk cologne from the night of the party when I bumped into him after I left the room.

Ring!

He put a finger up to his lips to be quiet, and I nodded in agreement as tears pooled into my eyes. He removed the phone from his pocket and answered.

"Do you have her?"

I started to scream when I recognized Addison's voice. I heard a deadly laugh over the phone.

"You have my money." His cold eyes bore into mine, and I gulped, feeling a tightness in my stomach. I made the worst mistake by not listening to Aydin and running back here alone.

"I have it. Bring her to me."

"Send me the address." He ended the call, reached back in his pocket, and pulled out a syringe. I tried to buck against him to get away, but then I felt a sharp poke to my neck and things blurred, slowly my eyes got drowsy and everything went black.

"Sleeping beauty."

* * *

SLOWLY, my eyes fluttered open, and my throat felt dry. I touched my forehead and closed my eyes again from the pounding migraine.

"How much did you give her?" I heard a woman's voice.

"Enough to keep her quiet to get her out of the building."

"Anyone see you?"

"No, I avoided all the cameras."

"Good. This bitch has caused more problems than I need."

"You know this will only bring on more problems." A third voice sounded familiar. I started to sit up when I felt a tightness on my wrist and saw handcuffs on both sides of me. I looked down and saw I was still dressed on top of a table.

"Arghhh." I tried to yank my hand again.

"How much time do you think it'll be before they come after her?"

"They won't find her," Addison spat.

"Please, let me go," I begged, trying to wiggle out of the chains.

The door opened, and all the people came in and focused on me.

"Are you hungry?" Tristan questioned, and Addison glared at him.

"She doesn't deserve food," Addison argued, stalked toward me, and slapped me across my face.

"Ahhh!" I groaned in pain, feeling blood pool into my mouth.

"You ruined everything. She doesn't get anything to eat!"

"Addison, let me go please."

"How long do you plan on holding her?" Tristan challenged, blowing out a breath.

"You just focus on getting my money into my account." Addison poked him in the chest.

"I told you it's complicated."

"Tristan, please help me," I pleaded, squeezing my eyes shut.

My heart pounded, glancing around the room at the blank walls. The room housed only the bed, with no windows.

"I'm in charge, Amelia, and I tried to warn you," Addison fussed, eyes narrowing into slits.

"Just let me go, and I'll leave town and forget this ever happened."

"Maybe we should let her go. I mean we can take the money and run," Tristan mentioned.

"Listen, we aren't leaving until I get my payback."

Addison placed her hands on her hips, cocked her head to the side.

"How long do you plan to keep her here?" Tristan questioned.

"I don't know yet." Addison crossed her arms over her chest, pacing back and forth.

The guy who kidnapped me admired me with lust-filled eyes.

"How long have I been here?" I prodded to get information.

"You ask too many questions. Listen to me clearly." Addison marched over, gripped my hair, and pulled my head to the side. I winced in pain, and she gripped her other hand around my neck, and started to choke me.

"He was mine! Do you know how long I've worked to get him?" she screamed and released her hand around my neck.

"Look, Addison, I'm not going to jail because you have some vendetta against her," Tristan warned. She glared at him.

"Tristan, you don't want to be on my bad side. Carlos, I need you to watch her," Addison informed him. I was nervous about being alone with him.

"That'll be extra," Carlos replied.

"Fine. I'll get you your money. She doesn't eat or drink."

"How do you think this is going to end, Addison?" Tristan grabbed her arm before she turned to leave, and Addison jerked out of his hold.

"It ends when I say it ends."

"What about me?"

"You'll get your money, Tristan. Let me figure something out. My accounts are frozen, so I need to rethink."

Addison and Tristan stepped out of the room, and Carlos approached me.

"Please, help me." Tears dripped down my cheek. He reached out and wiped them before they fell.

"You should have left it alone, little one."

Carlos removed a knife from his pocket, raised it to my cheek, and trailed it down my chest.

"I... I... swear, I won't say anything."

"I think she's got plans for you," he responded before removing the knife. He smiled and walked out of the room. I heard a lock on the door. I closed my eyes, sniffled, and cried for my family and Aydin to find me.

* * *

Two days later.

For the past two days, the only thing I'd been able to do was go to the bathroom and come right back to be locked up. I couldn't wash up, but he did give me food to eat even though Addison told him not to feed me. From what I gathered, she was trying to get money pulled together to leave the country because she was blasted in the media for stealing from her campaign. A few conversations I over-heard Carlos have, he stated that if she didn't have his money soon, he would make sure she was thrown under the bus.

"Has she always been in charge?" I watched Carlos lock me back up after I came from the bathroom. He paused and looked at me.

"Are you trying to do some mind games with me, little one?"

"No, I just want to understand."

"Nothing to understand. I was hired to do a job."

"What happens after they pay you?"

"I leave."

I chuckled.

"You think after you get your money, Addison is going to let you leave."

"She has no choice."

"Come on, you have to see she's crazy and only thinks about herself."

He pushed his hands in his pockets.

"Are you worried about my safety?" He smirked.

I rolled my eyes.

"I think you should let me go, and I won't testify against you."

"Ahhh. So let me get this straight—"

The door swung open, and Addison glanced from Carlos to me.

"What's going on here?" Addison sauntered in wearing a black pantsuit with her hair pulled up in a ponytail.

"Nothing," Carlos replied, winking at me.

"Doesn't seem like nothing." She pointed from me to Carlos.

"All you should worry about is my money."

"I'm calling the shots, Carlos. Remember that." She poked him in the chest.

"I asked him what happens after he gets his money," I blurted out. I felt if I could get them against each other, I might have a chance to escape.

"Did you now? Hmmm… seems like you're in my business again, Amelia Edwards." Addison tapped me on the cheek. I shifted my head away, and she jerked it back to stare in my eyes.

"Don't dismiss me, bitch!"

"Addison!" Carlos yelled. That was the first time he took up for me. Addison released me and stepped back.

"I don't recall telling you to have conversations with her."

"I run my business the way I see fit." Carlos walked off, and Addison stood in front of me.

"All you had to do was leave me alone."

"You're the one who came after me."

"My mistake was letting you go that night of the party."

"Aydin is going to find me."

"I doubt it."

"You think Tristan is going to stick around?"

"Tristan's an idiot; he'll do anything I ask."

"You might have him fooled, but Carlos sees the truth."

"Carlos won't betray me. Neither will Tristan. I still have support out here."

"You're all over the news, Addison. Think about this please."

"I have thought about everything, and you're going to pay."

"What does that mean?"

"Before you came into the picture, I was close to being in the position to have everything I ever wanted."

"If you stop and let me go, we can work something out."

Addison threw her head back and laughed.

"How would we work together? Do you think I'd put my life in your hands after I've held you hostage?" She pushed her finger in my face.

"I can talk to the police. Maybe we could get your help."

Her nostrils flared.

"I don't need help!"

"Okay. Okay."

"That's your problem now with the 'poor me' syndrome. Aydin probably feels sorry for you and knows how desperate you are to be loved."

"Aydin's not a part of this."

"Really, you think so?" She held a cocky expression.

My eyes drifted to the door.

"No one can save you."

"He's going to come for you."

"Then it means your family won't just lose you." Addison shifted and started to leave the room.

"Addison! Addison! Don't do this."

She stopped at the door with her back to me.

"It's already been done."

AYDIN

*D*ay before kidnapping.

We'd been in Chicago going through our list of contacts to find anything we could on Addison and Tristan. Our last visual was of them at a meeting with some investors at a hotel. We tracked down the list of companies she had dealings with after her father told us she wasn't answering his calls.

"Mr. Callahan, you donated up to ten thousand dollars, plus another fifty thousand into an account offshore," I read off from the form in front of me. At Callahan Investments, we faked like we had an appointment as potential customers to get a one-on-one.

"I'm not sure who you think you're dealing with, but you need to leave."

"Addison Chatsworth has been funneling money from her campaign for herself."

"What does that have to do with me?"

He stood in front of his desk.

"You've been spotted going into Lux Hotel here in

Chicago for quite some time and leaving a few minutes after her."

"My private life is none of your business."

"Correct, but when a senator is running for election and tries to have someone close to me killed, that becomes a problem for me."

"Whatever you have with Addison is your business."

"No see, that's where you're wrong."

I stared him in the eye.

"Addison and I have done work in the past."

"Do you think it's wise to lie to me?"

He peered from Nasir to me.

"She's a potential client, that's all."

"As the owner of a security firm, I make it my business to know potential threats, and you, sir, are becoming a threat I need to contain." I went around the desk and gripped him by the collar of his jacket.

"Ah!! Get your hands off me."

"What do you know about Addison Chatsworth?"

"Nothing! I've only invested with her from time to time."

"Don't lie to me."

"Her father connected us."

"Edgar's involved."

"All I know is that she's had ambitions of being in politics, even the White House."

"You helped her."

He shook his head.

"No, I only donated to her so it looks good."

"But all along, you've been helping her move money and tried to use my company when she brought in Tristan."

He looked at Nasir, then back to me, and I knew that was confirmation. I let him go.

"Addison is playing you."

"She's unstoppable. I tried to tell her it was too much too soon," he rambled on.

"Where does Edgar fit in with this situation?"

"As far as I know, he's blind to his daughter's situation. She has everyone thinking he's in charge, but she's running the entire operation."

"If we didn't come to Chicago last time, we probably set her on a course to come after Amelia full steam."

"We need to go by her place," Nasir remarked, and I nodded.

"If she calls you, I better be the first one you contact," I told him.

We cut him off, hopped in the van, and drove through downtown Chicago to her home in Glencoe. Something in my gut told me she wasn't to be trusted and that we should have broken ties a long time ago. Nasir hopped on the ninety-four freeway, and my cell buzzed with a text message.

Nicco: *2378 Addison's address, five thousand square feet gate.*

"She has a guard and gate," I said.

"How do you want to handle it?"

"We check it out and wait to hear from our contacts. I need to get back to Amelia."

He smirked.

"What is that smirk about?"

"You."

"Don't start."

"You've changed in a good way."

"I don't need this. I told you so."

"Yes, you do."

"She's different."

"I see, and the way you changed around her is good."

"At first, I was an asshole. I can admit that."

"The biggest asshole."

He nudged me in the arm, and we laughed.

"Fuck when the right woman comes around."

"True, makes you do things differently."

"How long do you think she'll stay before she wants to go back home?"

"She's probably planning to leave you right now and already packing," he joked.

"I have guards with her now, and Nicco told me he'd check in on her."

"Don't put too much pressure on her. Have her ready to run."

"She met my parents."

* * *

AN HOUR LATER, he stopped the car at the front gate of Addison's massive home and rolled the window down.

"Can I help you gentlemen?"

"We're a part of Addison's security team, and she wanted us to do a check of the premises before her event?" Nasir lied.

"What event? She hadn't informed me or anyone on her team."

"We're from TN Security?"

"Oh, I remember you've been here before with her father."

"Yeah, and to try to avoid her firing you and us, we just need about twenty minutes to check the area and create a report."

"When's the event?" He started to remove his phone.

"I'd rather not bug her with a phone call. You know how women get if we interrupt with simple questions."

He looked hesitant. Nasir removed his badge and showed him our ID.

"All right, twenty minutes." He stepped back and pushed the gate open. We drove up the winding driveway and parked. I stepped out and walked up to the door. Eloise, the house manager, who worked at her father's estate, opened the door.

"Mr. Nasir and Aydin. How can I help you?"

"Nice to see you again, Eloise. We're just doing a final check. Is Addison here?"

"No, she's in Tennessee with her father."

Nasir and I looked at each other.

"How long has she been gone?"

"I want to say almost a week."

"Did she say what she was going for besides her father?"

"No, she keeps her plans to a minimum."

"We won't interrupt you. We'll be out of your way," Nasir said, and I walked into her living room and peered around at the portraits of her family on the wall. Nasir came up around the corner.

"Check the office, and I'll go into her bedroom. She's bound to keep something lingering."

"You're right," I said and headed in the direction of her office. I pushed the door open and looked around at the pictures of her on the wall with other political leaders and celebrities. I checked over my shoulder, shut the door, strolled to the dresser drawer first, and opened it up. All her files were color coordinated and mostly her business files on the foundation. Nothing looked out of the ordinary. I shut it, moved to her desk, and turned on her computer. I saw she didn't have a password and went to her email. I scrolled through and noticed many messages between her and Tristan.

Addison: *I want the money moved now.*

Tristan: *I'm working on it. Give me time.*

Addison: *You have until the end of the week.*

Another group of emails from the night of the party showed an escalated conversation.

Tristan: *She saw us.*

Addison: *Who?*

Tristan: *Amelia, goddamn it!*

Addison: *She doesn't know anything.*

Tristan: *I'm not going down for this.*

Addison: *Keep your mouth shut.*

Tristan: *What if we go to jail?*

Addison: *No one will believe her.*

Tristan: *I knew this was a bad idea.*

Addison: *That money in your account sure changed your mouth.*

Tristan: *I'm out.*

Addison: *Calm down, Tristan. I'll take care of her.*

Tristan: *What does that mean?*

Addison: *It means Amelia won't be a problem for long.*

I grew more and more upset, ready to find Addison to answer some questions.

The door came open, and I looked up to see Nasir.

"We have to go."

"Why?"

"Have you checked your phone?"

"No. I put it on vibrate so we wouldn't be disturbed."

Nasir's face dropped.

"It's Amelia."

"What about her?" I jumped up and came around the desk.

"She's missing."

"What!" I reached in my pocket to grab my cell phone and saw missed calls from Nicco, Wesley, and Dani.

"Nicco called me after he tried to get in touch with you."

I dialed Nicco's number and ran out of the office with Nasir alongside me. We saw Eloise walk out of the kitchen.

"Addison just called," Eloise said, causing us to pause.

"What did you say?"

"Aydin! Aydin!" Nicco yelled my name over the line.

"She told me to tell you something, but I don't understand what it means."

"Just tell us." Nasir faced her.

"She said you won't miss her," Eloise repeated the message, and something inside me knew Addison had acted on her warning to Tristan.

"Aydin! Aydin!" I looked down at the phone and remembered Nicco on the other end.

"What you got?" I shifted toward the door and walked out, going to the driver's side of the car.

"Let me drive. You're not thinking clearly." Nasir tapped me on the back.

"I went to your place, and she wasn't there. I tried to call her but no answer," Nicco explained.

"Where was the guard I put on her?" I slammed the door, smashing a hand on top of the dashboard.

"He said she ditched him."

"Fuck!"

"Calm down, Aydin. We'll find her." Nasir tried to reassure me.

"Did you try her parents?" I questioned. Nasir started the car, pushed on the gas, and sped out of the driveway.

"They hadn't heard from her either."

"When was the last time you spoke to her?" Nasir probed.

I closed my eyes and thought back on our last conversation at dinner.

"We had dinner a few days after our last visit in Chicago."

"Let me see the phone." Nasir held out his hand.

"Nicco, get everyone assembled in the office. I want this a priority."

"Nicco, get Senator Edgar's last known phone records sent over to me," Nasir demanded, and I rubbed my hands together. If something happened to Amelia, that thought would have me ready to do something I wouldn't regret.

"We're on our way back." I ended the call.

"I know you're ready to kill, my brother, but I need you to be clear and not confused."

"Confused."

"You're in love, and that can be a dangerous thing."

"She emailed back and forth with Tristan about Amelia."

"You think she would be stupid enough to follow through?"

"With Addison, anything is possible."

"Those emails were clear about her intentions and the night of the party."

"When Amelia ran out?"

"Yeah, Amelia didn't even think we would believe her."

"She's going to be okay." Nasir put his hand on my shoulder.

"Something about this is different."

"What do you mean?"

"She knows we won't give up."

"She'd be stupid try to run."

"I need all of her family's addresses and any contacts in the police."

"On it."

"I need answers!" I shouted in the conference room. "She's been missing for too long, and I am ready to turn the entire city upside down. My men went to every location Amelia frequents, and I talked to her parents. They hadn't gotten a call or ransom for her return."

"We're leaning on everyone we can without making more noise," Nicco said.

"Then lean harder."

I launched all the papers across the table to the floor, my chest heaving up and down.

"Look, we need to relax and stay focused. Turning on the guys won't help." Nasir tried to talk me down.

"She's out there alone with some maniac and crazy bitch. Don't tell me to relax."

I got in Nasir's face, and Nicco stuck his hand between us to separate me.

"Amelia's strong."

"He's right, Aydin."

"All I want to know is how Addison slipped in with her men."

"She paid off the guard," Nicco confessed.

I blinked in disbelief.

"Where is he?"

"Take care of yourself. You don't need to worry about that." Nasir picked up the documents and placed them on the table.

"We know they took her from her apartment."

"And we have phone records between Addison and her dad," Nicco pointed out the sheets. Days of phone records revealed Addison only contacting her father once or twice, but everything else seemed normal as usual.

"She might have a second phone."

All eyes looked at me.

"What are you thinking?"

"In my mind, we underestimate Addison and think she's just some daughter of a rich politician."

"She has more goals and ambition," Nasir continued my statement.

"Right, she likes to play dumb, but I doubt her father is aware how far she's down the rabbit hole."

"Then let's inform him."

"We can do more than that."

"I think you're on to something." Nasir grinned.

"Tell the media."

"Get all news stations with the story."

"Wouldn't that cause Addison to get scared and run?" Nicco challenged.

"Not if she needs something," Nasir answered.

"She hasn't left the state. We have the airports tracked. Nothing in Chicago."

"So, we're sitting ducks?" Nicco inquired.

"No, we monitor the money, and the press will do the work for us."

"Show Addison in a light she's not used to so that the public will turn on her."

"She'll have no choice but to make an appearance."

"Then we'll have the upper hand, and she'll return Amelia," I said.

"While she's scrambling for cover."

"We track her movements and find her," I answered.

The team made the necessary calls, and I left the conference room back to my office and opened the door to the surprise of my father and brothers.

"What happened?"

"We wanted to check on you." Wesley stood and reached his arms out for a hug.

"Thanks, I'll be fine." I released him.

"You look like you haven't slept," Josiah mentioned, and I yawned at that moment because I'd been up all night, driving through the town and places I thought Addison would be.

"I can't sleep until she's back home."

"Any updates?" Dad wanted to know.

"None that pan out."

Wesley sat in the chair in front of my desk.

"I have the police on the case. If you need anything, let me know."

"Thanks."

"She's tough," Dad said.

"I know, but something just feels empty without her here."

"We brought you some food. Your mother wanted to come, but I told her you're busy." Dad lifted the bag of food from the table and laid it on my desk.

"I can't eat right now."

"You're not sleeping; at least eat to keep your strength up, son."

"He's right, Aydin. The only way you can help Amelia is to be alert and strong."

"I'm sure when Nasir gets any updates, he'll let you know." Josiah patted me on the back.

Ring!

The phone in my office lit up, and I looked up at my brothers and father. We'd been closed ever since I got word of Amelia missing and told everyone I'd contact them when we were back up and running.

"Who could that be?" Josiah asked.

I leaned forward, picking up the phone.

"You shouldn't have done this, Aydin."

Her whiny voice grated my ears.

"Where is she?"

"Is that all you think about?"

"Addison."

"No! She's not important. I am, and you're going to listen."

Wesley motioned with his hand to keep talking and typed on his phone.

"What do you want?"

"Now you want to talk to me." She laughed sarcastically.

"Whatever you think I've done, we can fix it."

"We would have been good together."

"Maybe, but you'll have to tell me where you are so we can talk."

"You think I'm stupid?"

"No."

"I'm not stupid, Aydin. My plan all along was to become more powerful, then we would have been the biggest power couple in the world."

"It can still happen."

"No, because your so caught up with this dumb bitch!"

"Where's Amelia?"

"She's tied up right now. I can take a message." She giggled through the phone.

I bit my bottom lip to stop from going off and making things worse for Amelia.

"I talked to your father."

"He's going to understand."

"Are you sure? I mean have you looked at the news lately?"

"That was your fault! Everyone thinks I'm crazy."

"Tell me where you are Addison, and we can talk in person."

"So you can try to save your precious woman." She had an evil laugh.

"Bitch! When—"

The call dropped before I could finish, and I threw it across the desk. Nasir rushed into my office.

"We got her."

I jumped up and followed him.

"Be safe, Aydin!" Dad called out.

"I'm with you, bro," Wesley remarked.

"Me too," Josiah suggested.

"Stay here and keep an eye on things." I opened the locker, removed a weapon, and picked up a vest. The rest of my men strapped up with ammo, jackets, and binoculars.

"He's right. We need people here in case something happens while we're gone," Nasir said.

We jogged outside to the awaiting black vans and hopped in. I put on the earpiece and the monitor of Addison's location.

"How many men does she have?"

"I got one on the inside and three outside. It's an abandoned building," Nasir stated.

"This is near downtown Memphis," I muttered, looking at the entrance of the building with men standing guard.

"How do you want to approach?" Nasir picked my brain.

"You and I take the back, and Nicco takes the front with his team."

"Make sure you avoid shooting anyone, unless it's necessary."

"Until we have eyes on Amelia, we can't go in guns blazing."

"I hear you," Nicco answered.

"How did you trace her?"

"Nicco was able to tap into our phone line, and it pinged off the tower and matched the last digits of the number."

"She was calling from a bogus number."

"Not too bright, but we cut the ten numbers down and located where it's from."

"Save her for me," I demanded, as thoughts of how she had been treating Amelia filled my head.

"Here's another little surprise that went out." Nasir scrolled through the monitor and showed me a news report of Addison.

"We have breaking news that Addison Chatsworth is on the run after being accused of kidnapping," the reporter from KBNF said.

"Her father sent a notice that the accusations are baseless," Nicco mentioned, and I figured he'd want to save face.

"Too late to try to save her now. She made her bed."

The car turned down Beale Street, and the driver turned off the lights a few blocks from the destination.

"Remember, try not to kill anyone until I find her."

I slid the door open, climbed out, and checked to make sure my gun was on me. I waved and pointed for Nicco to take the lead and motioned for the alley I was going through a block from the building. Behind me, Nasir shifted and got my attention. Someone was smoking in the alley. I wiggled my finger, balled my fist up, and slid against the wall before he turned to see me. I caught him around the neck and whispered in his ear, "If you scream, I'll kill you." I held him in a headlock as he tried to get loose.

I tightened my grip and threw him to Nasir, who punched him in the throat. I walked up to the back door of the building and saw it was locked. I pulled my gun out with the silencer and shot the lock off. Slowly, I pulled the door open and noticed it was empty and grew frustrated. Continuing to hold the gun up in front of me and trailed down the dark hallway. Finally, Nasir caught up to me, and we looked at each other and saw a light on in a room. I pointed to myself indicating I would go first and slightly pushed it ajar. I saw no one inside, but a TV played a game show.

"This is the place," Nasir whispered, and I believed him, but it was more like a distraction to throw us off.

"There's about twenty floors here."

"She wouldn't have men outside unless this was the place."

"I have to think," I said.

"What if we're being watched?"

"What do you mean?"

"She knew we'd trace the call."

"So, this is a chase to make us go crazy."

"Edgar."

"Edgar."

I nodded.

"The last place we'd think she would keep someone is her father's place."

"She would be stupid to her at her father's home.."

"If her father had multiple homes, he wouldn't know."

"I have the addresses of the main home and a few condos in the city."

"Which one has the most privacy?"

"You're right," Nasir said.

"Tell me."

He held the phone in front of me with a satellite visual of the property.

"A cabin on the outskirts of the city behind the woods."

"The perfect place to escape." I texted Nicco the address and said we're out. We went back out the way we came in, jogged to the van, and climbed back in to leave.

* * *

THIRTY MINUTES LATER, we arrived a mile from the condo, approaching a rocky road that led up to a path with a No Trespassing sign. Nicco turned the car off, and we looked at the map of the area.

"They'll know we're here by now," Nicco said.

"We have to go on foot from here," I replied, unlocked the van, and grabbed the bags of explosives.

"If we're going in, make sure we stay in contact with each other."

"Nicco, you take the explosives and start some fireworks. When they come out, we shoot anyone who's not Amelia," I commanded.

"Got it, boss."

"He's back."

"He never left."

I grabbed the shotgun and cocked it back with the scope attached.

"You have three minutes," Nicco informed us, and we took off to run through the grass and behind the sign. I jogged, looked at my watch, and counted down to the three-minute mark.

Boom!

"Go!" I shouted and ran toward the cabin with my gun ready when men came outside yelling and ran toward the fire.

Bang! Bang!

I shot two men, and Nasir sliced another with his knife. Another guy sent a shot our way, and I dropped to the ground.

Pop! Popppp!

"Stay down!" I yelled. Nasir pulled his gun out and sent shots back toward them.

"Take the left side!" He scrambled and jumped up, and I followed to watch his back.

Boom!

Another explosive went off, and I knew Nicco was on his way to back us up. I ran up the stairs and kicked the door inside, and a man tried to jump up with his gun.

"If you want to live, I would put that gun down."

His eyes glanced to the right, and I followed when he tried to shoot, but my gun went off first.

"Arggh!" he screamed.

"Told you not to try me." I looked from my right to left, Nasir was behind me, and I checked the side door, but no one was inside.

"Help! Help!"

I heard screams.

"She's here." I took off running.

AMELIA

arlos was in the front, talking to someone on the phone, and Addison was with Tristan somewhere around here, discussing about moving me to somewhere else. I didn't know what spooked them but me not being locked up here became a problem. I'd already eaten before Addison came, and Carlos let me use the restroom to wash up and brush my teeth. I thanked him for that gesture, but he was still just as guilty as her for keeping me here.

Click!

The door opened, and Carlos stood behind Addison.

"What's going on?"

"We're leaving," Addison spoke.

"Why?"

"You don't ask questions."

Addison waited for Carlos to unlock my wrists as she held a gun to my head.

"Try anything, and you're dead."

"Addison, this has gone on too long."

"Don't worry, you'll see Aydin again... in hell." She

grabbed me by the arm, yanked me off the bed, and dragged me.

"Help! Help!" I screamed and tried to kick away. When Carlos smacked me across the face, I fell backwards and held my cheek.

"Next time, think twice about testing me." Addison stood over me with a gun.

Pop!

"Ughhh." I gasped as Carlos's body dropped to the ground. I looked up and saw Aydin with a gun trained on Addison.

"Aydin!" I shouted, trying to run to him. She grabbed me with the gun to my back and her arm around my neck.

"Stay back!" Addison shouted.

"Addison, it's over," Aydin said.

"Aydin, we could have been good together."

"If you want to walk out of here, let her go."

"She's my insurance."

"I can't let you do that."

"Where's Tristan?"

"He's dead," Aydin answered.

I felt Addison stiffen at the response.

"You're lying." Her voice cracked.

"It's all over the news that you paid your way out of this with family money."

"All you care about is her."

"Arghhh!" She grabbed my hair and yanked my head back.

"Addison!" Another voice screamed, and I took that chance to step on her foot and dropped down to the ground.

Pop! Poppppp!

I covered my ears and closed my eyes.

"You're safe, baby," he whispered in my ear and held me in his arms.

"Aydin." I sniffed, trying to hold in my tears.

"Let's go. We have company," Nasir spoke, and I finally realized who the voice matched.

"Who's here?" Aydin picked me up in his arms, and I buried my face in his neck.

"The news." Nasir removed his jacket and covered it over my face.

"Tell Nicco to bring the car up closer."

"Already did it. He has the other truck blocking the entrance," Nasir responded, I peered out behind him and saw the van's door open.

"Is Tristan really dead?"

"Yeah. He was hiding in a closet with a gun," Nasir answered.

"Come on, it's nothing for you to worry about." Aydin kissed the top of my head and helped me climb in the van, strapped me in, and sat next to me.

"I just want to go home."

"Did they hurt you?"

"She wouldn't let me eat or shower, but Carlos allowed it when she wasn't around."

"I wish I could kill her again."

"It's over now."

"I'll take you to the hospital."

"I'm fine."

"No, you've been dehydrated and malnourished."

"Okay."

"Listen to me."

"I know."

"There's nothing I wouldn't do to protect you."

He held my hand.

"I know." He pressed a kiss on my lips, leaned his arms on the back of the seat, and pulled me into his chest.

"Sleep. We'll be at the hospital soon."

* * *

A FEW DAYS later in the hospital.

I smiled up at the nurse as she checked my vitals, and Aydin sat at the edge of the bed, running a hand up my leg in comfort. I was being discharged today after all the tests came back negative. Aydin had security outside the door and the building in case any of the Chatsworths tried to come up here and do anything. It was all over the news about my captivity, and reporters tried to call the hospital line and pay nurses to get them inside my room. One tried to steal my trash, and Aydin told the hospital he would sue if anything personal was leaked. They stopped then. I thanked her for letting the bed up and pushed the tray of food in front of me.

"I'll eat when I get home."

"You need to have something in your stomach." I learned her name was Sasha when she cursed out one reporter that tried to sneak up here, and we became close.

"I'll make sure she eats." Aydin grinned, and I rolled my eyes. At night, he avoided snuggling with me in the bed. I told him I was fine, but he worried over every little thing I had taken. I told him to release it because it was my own fault for not listening.

"Thank you, Mr. Reeve." Sasha walked out of my room and a second later, it opened with my parents walking in with balloons.

"She's awake," Mom cheered and reached over to hug me. Dad placed the balloons and a bear on the table under the TV.

"I told you I'd be home soon."

"We figured we'd come and help if you needed a ride or something."

"I have Aydin all ready to chauffeur me around."

"Did the doctor say you're good to leave?" Dad asked.

"Yes, Dad. Don't worry," I huffed out. He reached over to pick up my hand.

"You're our baby. We'll always worry." He kissed me on the forehead.

"Aydin, have you heard any news about the people who did this to our daughter?" Mom questioned.

"It's being handled, I promise."

"Stop stressing, you two. Did you cook?" I asked.

"I can once you get home," Mom answered, and I looked over at Aydin.

"She's staying at my place," Aydin responded.

"Temporarily," I said.

Aydin pressed his lips in a thin line, brows narrowed to slits.

"Maybe you should come stay with us. You don't want to burden Aydin." Mom rubbed my shoulder.

"I promise I'm fine. My apartment is getting cleaned up, and I'll be back home soon."

The nurse returned with my discharge papers, and I signed off on everything, climbed out of bed, and went to the bathroom to change. Fifteen minutes later, I felt refreshed and brand-new after throwing on a little gloss and combing my hair. Dani brought a pair of jeans and a t-shirt from my closet and a pair of flats.

"The car's ready." Aydin stood behind the wheelchair.

"I forgot I have to leave in that."

"We'll follow you." Mom picked up my bags, and I grabbed my coat and purse.

"Have you thought about what you're going to do for work?"

Dad called for the elevator, and we stood in awkward silence.

"I'm planning to open my own business."

Ding!

I could see the grimace across Aydin's face through the elevator doors at the surprise announcement.

"What type of business?"

"It's an agency that will handle office needs. I had a great time as operations manager at his business. I thought I could do it for other people."

"With what money, baby?" Mom asked.

"I'll take out a loan."

"That's a lot of work." Dad stepped off the elevator first. Aydin pushed me through the double doors, and I saw Nasir at the awaiting SUV and smiled.

"Nasir!" I waved, and he hopped out of the car, came around to hug me, and helped get my things in the car.

"Are you ready to break out of here?" Nasir joked.

"You have no idea. This one has not stopped with all his questions for the doctor."

Aydin shut the door and climbed in the front seat. My parents placed my things in the back, kissed me, and walked off to their car. I knew they'd have questions about my life choices and changes, but I couldn't dwell on what happened forever. I was healed now or at least safe from harm. Nasir drove out of the hospital parking lot and stared out the window at the city lights. I could breathe a sigh of relief and feel the anguish of being locked up no longer.

"Can we stop at my place?"

"Why?"

"I wanted to see if anything needs to be replaced."

"You can do that later, but you're moving in permanently."

"Aydin," I groaned and threw my head back on the seat.

"No arguments. I need to know you're safe at all times."

"We'll discuss it later."

Thirty minutes later, we pulled up to his home, and I noticed a few cars parked in his driveway and on the block. He came around and helped me out of the car.

"I'm fine, babe." I leaned into his arms and kissed him on the mouth, sucking on his bottom lip. He caressed my ass and groaned into my mouth.

"Save that until after I leave." Nasir cleared his throat, and I pulled back.

"Sorry." I grabbed Aydin's hand, and we walked into his house.

"Surprise!" I jumped back.

My mouth dropped open at everyone from the office and my parents here with a large sign that said Welcome Home.

"When did you do this?"

Aydin wiped the tear from my left cheek.

"Dani planned it when I told her we found you."

Dani ran over and hugged me.

"So glad you're safe," Dani said.

"Me too, you didn't have to do all of this, Dani."

"Yes, we did. You're my best friend," Dani responded and motioned at the buffet of food on the table.

"Wow. You guys went all out."

"I only do things big and dramatic," Dani joked and picked up a tray of my favorite snacks: Oreo cookies, Thin Mints, and salt and vinegar chips.

"You need to eat first, Amelia." Mom held a plate of food in front of me.

"You cooked!" I reached over to hug her.

"Of course I did. I knew we wouldn't convince you to stay with us, but your father wanted to try one more time." Mom winked at me.

I chuckled at Dad and Mom being in Aydin's house and driving him crazy for the last few days without me as a buffer.

"Sit and eat." Aydin helped me over to the couch, and I talked with Molly and a few co-workers.

"Did you ever fill out a police report?" Dani poured me a glass of wine, and I sipped it.

"I talked to the police. His brother is on the force." I pointed at Wesley in the corner, next to Aydin.

"I still can't believe Addison kidnapped you," Molly expressed, and everyone muttered in agreement.

"Addison and Tristan."

"Let's move on. This will only take you to a dark place," Dani said.

"Yes, when are you coming back to the office?" Molly asked.

"I'm not."

"That means I'll be alone again."

I giggled at the sorrowful expression on her face.

"I'll stop in from time to time, but I have a new thing I want to pursue."

"Please spill." Dani poured herself more wine.

"I'm starting my own business that handles operations management positions for different companies."

"That sounds interesting," Molly said.

"I know, and it's because of you and your encouragement. The work of an office manager to a higher scale."

"Let me know if you need any help."

"I promise to keep you updated."

We laughed and talked all day until everyone left. Aydin helped me shower and get into bed, and we cuddled up together. We hadn't slept together or even thought of doing anything sexual since I'd been back, and I appreciated him for his care and kindness with not only my mind, but body.

"What do you have to do tomorrow?" I rubbed a hand up and down his chest.

"A few meetings, but nothing that will take the whole day."

"I'm going to check out a few buildings with Dani."

"You're serious about the business idea."

"Yes. How do you feel about me no longer being at the security firm?"

He sighed and moved his left hand behind his head.

"Not happy, but I understand why you need your space."

"Not from you. It's just a way to gain my independence."

"I get it, MeMe."

"You and this nickname." I laughed.

"You don't like it?" Aydin pulled his arm down and lifted my chin to peck my lips.

"I like anything you call me."

"I suggest you get some sleep before I have you entangled in my bed and screaming my name."

"Only if it's for pleasure."

* * *

THE NEXT DAY.

Dani pulled up to the Angel's Café and headed toward the hostess station at the door. I waved for her to notice me at the table. She came over, bent down, hugged me, then sat across with the menu in front of her.

"You looked refreshed." I lifted the water jug to pour a glass for her and then myself.

"I had a good sleep after the party."

"A good sleep with a sexy man."

She pushed her lips together for a kiss and grinned.

"Shussssh." I took a sip of my water, and the server approached our table.

"Hello, I'll be your server. My name is Todd." He pulled out a pen and paper.

"Can I get the tuna melt and side salad, plus onion rings," Dani ordered.

"I'll have the same." I gathered my menu and passed it to him.

"And to drink?"

"Coke is fine."

"Arnold Palmer for me," I answered.

Todd picked up our menus and left us alone at the table.

"Give me the details on this business."

"Nothing major, but I found a spot not far from Aydin's firm."

"You ready to take on the responsibility?"

"I mean, it'll be like any business."

"Yeah, but you've always worked for other people."

"Once the paperwork is filed, I'll figure out the hiring team, since Aydin wants me to stay with him. That could save me money on bills."

"You're thinking of permanently living with him?"

"I was hesitant in the beginning, you know, but the way he's given me space and opened his home, I'm considering it."

"You're in love."

I smiled and covered my face, feeling like a teenager with her first boyfriend in high school.

"Obviously we're committed, and he's changed from the asshole I first met."

Todd arrived with our drinks and salad.

"Thank you."

Dani sipped on her drink.

"If you need anything, let me know."

"I wouldn't put you out like that. I'm good."

"Well, tell me about this Addison woman."

"She's gone, thank God, but I'm thankful for Aydin and his team."

"She took you from your apartment and tried to have you killed." Dani shook her head in despair.

"Stop… I don't want you to go down that rabbit hole I was on."

"It's hard."

She wiped her tears.

"I underestimated her; she was tougher than I thought."

"That bitch, if she were alive, I'd kick her ass."

I chortled at her response.

"How about we leave her in the past, and you come check out my building I found."

Dani agreed, and we continued to talk and catch up as the food was brought out to the table. Two hours later, we pulled up to the office I'd planned to open in a few months. The building was in a quiet business district, a few blocks from Aydin, so we'd be able to have lunch whenever we wanted.

"It's cute." Dani met me at the entrance, and I unlocked the door. The building was a standalone two-story office building with three offices and two bathrooms. There was a small parking lot on the corner of the building.

"I can't wait to decorate."

Dani scanned the office door in the corner.

"That'll be my office, and I'll hire an assistant and two employees."

"I think maybe a light gray and cream color scheme would work. Open space." Dani opened the blinds in the front of the entrance.

"All planned out."

"Proud of you, my friend."

"Thank you. I've come a long way."

"Soon, your name will be in lights." Dani twirled in a circle.

I cackled and clapped my hands.

"Just think, we could have lost you."

She sadly turned to me.

"You'll never have to worry about that again."

We hugged and wiped our tears away and headed out of the office. Locking up, I walked to my car and decided to hang with my parents for a few hours before I head home. My new normal included a man who treated me like I was gold and wanted the best for me without anything in return. I reversed out of the parking lot, honked at Dani, and drove down the street, turning on the old-school classic rock music with thoughts of my business venture.

AYDIN

A month later.

Many women would say I'd been closed off and avoided a relationship altogether, but Amelia opened me up to the idea of what my parents had. After Addison and Tristan were killed, I let my grip ease up, and we decided to go on a little retreat. Nasir was in charge of the office while we were away, and I reveled in what I was to do with the full curves that stood in front of me.

"What are you doing?" She glanced up while I untied her robe. The beach cabin I brought us to was secluded, and I could have her any way I wanted without interruptions. Her heavy breasts, in the thin corset, called for me to squeeze. Her legs looked longer in the high heels, and the white color against her skin spurred me on to kiss her on the lips gently.

"Taking in this moment." Amelia stood on her toes and grasped my chin, plunging her tongue in my mouth. I grabbed her around the waist and walked her backwards against the wall.

"Mmmm… I'm going to make you beg all night long." I

eased my tongue across her shoulder, up to her neck, and teased her ear with a light bite, licking the sting away. My palm grazed her stomach down to her sweet heat, and I stuck one finger inside. She arched against the wall and dropped her head against my chest. With each dip in her pussy, I explored how she succumbed to my lead. She spread her legs further to give me access, and I removed my finger and stuck it in her mouth, then mine. She held me tight, and I dropped my shorts, lifted her, and eased in with her wrapped around my neck. Amelia whimpered against my neck, and I buried myself in deep. She palmed the back of my head, and I groaned at the sweet juices drizzling down my thighs.

"Arghhh... mmmmm." Amelia ran her hand up and down my back. Our hearts beat in sync. She panted, out of breath, when I gripped her breasts.

"So lucky to have you, baby." The love and praise I'd come to appreciate about her, I promised to continue until the day we died.

"I no longer have to dream about you in my arms." Amelia brushed her lips over mine.

"No more dreams. This is us together forever."

I pulled us away from the wall and placed her in the middle of the bed, still tangled together while I slowed down and made love to her until we both passed out.

"WHAT THE FUCK!" My eyes popped open at the feel of her warm lips wrapped around my dick. We hadn't gone to sleep until around three in the morning after we showered and had sex, then changed the sheets. I turned my head and saw it was going on eleven in the morning. I peeked down at Amelia staring back at me.

"Ughhh..." I sat up and pushed her hair to the side, to see her plump lips take me down her throat.

"Mmmm..." she moaned. I reached over and smacked her ass.

"Come sit on him."

This was our last day in Jamaica and even though I could stay in bed all day, I knew she wanted to explore a little more.

"My favorite morning treat."

Two hours later, we showered again and ordered breakfast. We finally came out of the cabin to sightsee and take pictures.

"I want to say something." Amelia stopped and turned toward me.

"Go ahead." I stretched my arm around her neck.

"Promise me you'll never allow anyone to come between us."

"I promise you forever."

We kissed and held hands, heading to the end of the beach to get on the boat I rented. I helped her step on and passed the blanket and basket to hold when I stepped on. On the back of the boat, I had an area set up with flowers and champagne to drink.

"Mr. Reeve, we have you all set." The captain shook my hand, and I thanked him.

"I don't think I want to ever leave here." Amelia looked over the clear blue water and smiled. The crew started the boat, and I opened the basket and placed the food containers on the floor. I leaned forward, cupped her chin, and paused to look in her eyes.

"We can come back."

"I know you're going to be busy traveling." I grabbed a fork and knife, as she popped the champagne bottle and poured us a small amount. Before I took the step to commit, my life was chaotic and only about work. Now, it was stillness by being with Amelia, and a part of me wanted this responsibility of being in her life.

"What do you want to do after this?"

The sun bounced off her skin, and I leaned forward and kissed her shoulder.

"Maybe a swim."

"We can do that."

"Are you still going with Nasir to open the New York office?" Amelia cut into her pasta salad and slid it in her mouth.

"For about a month or two."

"I'll miss you."

"You can come with me."

"No, I want to do my own thing, and I'm close to doing that now."

I understood her wanting to have independence and creating her own lane with a business of her own. At first, she was hesitant to take my money, but she got over it quickly when I made sure she knew I wouldn't have anything to do with the work that she did.

"You'll never have to worry or stress again about Addison or her family."

"I can't believe she tried to kill me."

"We've dealt with a lot of crazy killers before, but to have it so close to home was eye opening."

"All right, we're on vacation. Let's forget about the Chatsworths and focus on us."

"I like the way your mind works."

"I knew you'd see it my way."

Amelia picked up a strawberry and fed it to me.

* * *

Two days later, I was in the office with my team, going over updates. Amelia was at her office, and I had security through her building, plus cameras inside and out to watch everyone who came and went. At first, she tried to protest, but my priority was her safety.

"So, I will take on two cases this week." Nasir passed the case file over to me.

"Who are we monitoring?"

"One of my contacts at the CIA said we need to extract a witness."

"Do you trust this contact?"

"Hard to say."

"I think you should take backup."

"Montana," Nicco remarked.

"I'm not sure we should take the job."

"What are you thinking?"

"We have to factor in what this witness knows," I said.

"I'll do a little more digging," Nasir announced and closed the file.

Nicco and I talked as we headed out of the conference room when I heard loud yelling. I followed the noise to the front entrance of the office and saw Senator Edgar in Amelia's face.

"Can I help you with something, Senator?"

I pulled Amelia behind me.

"I want her arrested."

"Your daughter's the reason for how she ended up!" Amelia shouted, then Edgar tried to reach over and grab her.

"Senator or no senator, never in your life try to put your hands on her." I gritted my teeth and pushed him back. His security tried to get in the middle, but Nicco and Nasir stopped them.

"I came up here to surprise you with lunch, and he saw me talking to Molly," Amelia started, and I released Edgar.

"Addison was right about you." Edgar reached in his pocket and pulled out his phone.

"Addison was sick, and she tried to kill her and me."

"One phone call, and I can have her arrested." Edgar shook his phone in my face.

"Do that, and your career will be over, Senator."

"Are you threatening me?"

"I promise you'll regret that call."

"I buried my child because of that woman!"

"I gave all of the information to the police already."

"You probably doctored the information."

I glanced at Amelia, then Nasir and I made eye contact.

"Senator, I'm telling you for the last time, we'll never speak on this again."

"I know you're about to open more businesses. I wonder how that will happen when I tell all of my contacts about you," Edgar taunted and stuffed his phone back in his pocket.

"Try me."

My fists balled up automatically.

"This won't be over."

He marched out of the building.

"Sorry to cause you more grief." Amelia grasped my hand, and I pressed a kiss on top of her head.

"It's not your fault."

"Yes, it is."

"No, you did your job."

"Ughh… I hate this feeling."

"What feeling?"

"Like he's going to cause more drama than his daughter."

"You don't have to worry about him." I interlocked our

hands, as we walked into my office. I walked to my desk and opened the drawer. Edgar thought I didn't have leverage after everything we went through with his crazy daughter. He didn't know what I was capable of doing.

"What's that?" Amelia set the bags of food on the table.

"Edgar."

"Huh?"

I passed her the file and sat next to her on the couch. Amelia flipped it open, and I watched as her eyes widened in shock.

"He's money laundering for the mob?"

"Yep, and if he does anything to you, then I'll have to get this over to my friends at the SEC and FBI."

"Do you think that's where Addison got this from?"

I shrugged.

"Probably, but I will never know."

"Glad you're on my side, Aydin Reeve." She cupped both sides of my face and leaned forward for a kiss.

"Me too."

She pecked my lips twice.

"So, how's the business going?"

"Great. I have almost everything set up. I need a few more pieces for the office."

"If you need anything—"

"I know where to go." She smirked and tapped her thigh.

"Long as you know."

"Dinner tonight with the guys?"

"I can't. I have a mission to prepare for."

"Where?"

"Can't tell you that."

"Something dangerous?"

"Everything I do is dangerous, baby." I pulled her onto my lap.

"Well, Mr. Dangerous, as long as you're protecting yourself."

"The guys always have my back."

"And you have theirs."

"Until my last breath."

"You're a good man, Aydin Reeve."

"From your lips, baby."

"How long will you be gone?"

"Not sure, but I want you to listen to the security in charge."

"My babysitter."

She pouted, and I tapped her nose.

"Your guard. Don't make me punish you." I rubbed her right butt cheek.

"Maybe I want you to punish me," she cooed and pressed her chest against me.

"Woman."

"Yes, Mr. Reeve."

"Are you trying to turn me on?"

"Is it working?"

"Just your presence turns me on, baby."

I smashed my lips against her mouth and rubbed a hand up her back. She groaned in my hold, and we made out for the rest of the lunch hour. The day she stumbled across my path was the day I became alive. When everything was against us, we prevailed, and I couldn't wait to see how things would be in a few years.

EPILOGUE:

AYDIN

Two years later.

The building housed the latest equipment with our logo up high on the top, while more staff brought in furniture that I had ordered. TN Security had four locations now, and I was busier than ever and enjoyed what I did for a living. I couldn't wait to branch off even more. I heard giggling from my office and went to see what the commotion was about. I saw my mom and Amelia in a huddle together. She'd been doing better mentally and physically since Edgar tried once again to disturb our peace and got her arrested. He'd doctored up a whole story, and the police went along with his word, and she spent a few weeks behind bars. When it came to Amelia, I lost all sense and barged in his office to kill him. Thankfully, Nasir was with me and pulled me off him. The files were sent to the FBI, and he was brought up on charges and arrested and was now sitting in prison awaiting trial.

"Shouldn't you two be working?"

I stalked over and kissed my mom on her cheek, then Amelia on the lips.

"She reminded me that I should get you one of those picture frames with all your brothers."

"I like my office, Mom. I'd rather not destroy it with your sons."

"All of my boys are handsome." Mom pinched my cheek.

"Yeah, Aydin, your brothers are cute," Amelia teased, and I glared.

"Why are you looking at them?"

"Someone sounds jealous." Amelia bit her bottom lip.

"He's like his father but never wants to admit it though."

"Dad gets jealous over you?"

"When does he not?" She motioned her hand in the air.

"I've noticed that with all the Reeve men." Amelia wrapped another picture of us together in Jamaica.

"The only man you need to worry about is me." I grabbed her around the waist.

"No funny business, Aydin." Amelia wiggled out of my arms.

"Mom understands," I joked.

"Yeah, that's why I have three boys," she answered, and I pretended to gag.

"I don't need that visual in my head."

"So, you have a Tennessee office, New York, Chicago, and now California. What's next for you?"

Mom inquired, removing the empty box from my desk.

"Another vacation."

"You're going to be too busy to vacation," Amelia commented.

"Amelia, how is your business going?" Mom asked.

"Great. I have five clients now." Amelia plugged in the phone.

"I think it's wonderful that you started your own business." Mom left the trash by the door.

"He encouraged me, and now a lot of his clients come to me for a referral."

Knock!

"Aydin! Are you ready?" Nasir stood at my open door.

"Yeah."

"Where are you going?" Amelia questioned.

"A little business."

"Is this business going to have you gone all day and night?" Amelia clasped her arm with mine, walking me toward the door.

"No, so make sure you cancel any plans with Dani."

"I'll finish up here and meet you at home." Amelia extended her arm around my neck. I bent down to kiss her on the lips.

"Don't be late," she muttered through our kiss.

"I won't."

Nasir pulled the keys from his pocket and pushed the front door open. I stepped around the passenger side, climbed in, and closed my eyes to relax.

"You ready for this?" Nasir started the car and pulled out of the parking lot.

"He wanted to talk to me. This is a courtesy visit."

Edgar didn't realize the weight of his mistakes until afterwards, and I made sure my contacts inside the jail kept me informed of everything he was doing. He'd pressed for me to come and visit him because he had something to tell me. At first, I declined. One thing I'd always remembered was to keep your enemies close, and he was a problem before, so I hoped he'd take my advice and do his twenty years without any disruption.

* * *

The guard escorted him in and nudged him to take a seat. He looked like he'd lost a few pounds after being locked up for a year. He cleared his throat.

"Why did you request to see me?"

"Straight to the point."

Any emotions I had for what I did to his daughter left the second she tried to make it seem like we were more than employees and clients.

"I'm not here to sit and apologize."

"Didn't think you'd be so arrogant," he spat sarcastically.

I lifted my wrist to look at the time.

"You have one minute before I get up and leave."

"All right, I wanted to tell you that what Addison did was wrong."

"You understand now that you're in jail." I shook my head.

"Look, we can help each other out."

He looked behind him and to the left as the other guards stood watch.

"How so?"

"I can give you names of people who had a hand in what I was doing."

"You mean like the mob?"

Edgar nodded.

"It's deeper than you think."

"Why are you telling me this and not the police or your lawyer?"

"Because… Because I need a favor." He leaned forward and whispered.

"I'm not in the business of doing you any favors."

"Just hear me out."

As crazy as it sounded, I could use him for my benefit and get more criminals off the street. Only he'd want something in return, and I wouldn't go for him getting out after a year.

"First, tell me what you have."

"The things I know could get me killed, and I need safety or to get out of here."

I waved off his suggestion.

"You're not getting out of here."

"If you put in a good word with the warden, I know I'd get a lesser sentence."

"That all depends on what you have."

"The people behind the money I was laundering aren't happy with you."

"I don't care."

"It's not safe for me or you, let alone your family."

"My family will be safe. Can you say the same?"

"Okay, I just need to think about what my next move is going to be."

"When you figure it out, I'll be back, and it better be worthwhile." I stood and turned my back to leave. Edgar thought I'd have some sympathy for him, so I walked through the prison's front entrance and got back in the car with Nasir.

"How did it go?"

"Like I thought it would."

"He tried to bribe you?"

I removed my phone from my pocket, went to the recording on my phone, and hit replay.

"*I can give you names of people who had a hand in what I was doing.*" I held the phone up for Nasir to listen.

"That sounds like we might need to look into this cartel a little further."

"We can research a little more before we make a decision."

"Are you going to tell Amelia about this update?"

EPILOGUE:

"As much as I know without worrying her."

"If I haven't told you, I'm proud of you, man."

"Why?"

"Your mood has changed. You smile more." He laughed, and I flipped him off.

Buzz!

I looked down and saw Amelia's text message scroll across.

Amelia: *I love and miss you.*

"Get me home."

"Something wrong?"

"Everything's right." He knew my intention and welcomed the calm Aydin as brothers in arms. We'd seen some bad things. The moment we found some peace, we didn't want anything to interrupt it and send us in a different direction. I found my sunshine through the storm, and her name was Amelia Edwards, and I couldn't wait to see what our future held.

* * *

I hope you enjoyed Amelia and Aydin. Check the sneak peek of "**Nasir**" on the next page. Follow my standalone opposites attract, age gap, military romance "**Exposed**" https://books2read.com/u/bQyYZe . Are you a fan of sports romance? Then download one-night stand, billionaire romance "**Refuel**" https://books2read.com/u/boDyDA. Also, follow it up with workplace, sports romance "**Pressure**" https://books2read.com/u/3Ly1r7 .If you love romantic comedy, fake relationships, enemies to lovers, find it here, "**Something Gained**." Click the link https://books2read.com/u/baGLYy .

Please also check out a second-chance, workplace romance here, "**Heart of Stone Book 4**" https://book-

190

s2read.com/u/4NXyPG with a host of characters intertwined.

Follow Desiree and Gabriel in *"Temptation"* a stand-alone contemporary, sports, curvy girl romance. Check it out here https://books2read.com/u/mle1Vv

Check out mafia romance here, ***"Antonio and Sabrina Book 1"*** https://books2read.com/u/4AxKLo

Any fan of forbidden romance, political? Check out **"Mutual Agreement"** https://books2read.com/u/mgzzWX a steamy romance. Pre-order the full novel of **"Nasir"** here click the link here.

Have you checked out **"She's All I Need"** click here https://books2read.com/u/49lkeW a sports, opposites attract romance. What about dark romance that has everything from steamy romance, opposites attract, suspense, thriller, celebrity, and more **"Joaquin Fuertes Book 1"** https://books2read.com/u/mvZlgV

Catch up with favorite characters in this holiday short romance which includes spoilers. https://books2read.com/u/bzd59G

SNEAK PEEK: NASIR

Chloe is used to the limelight, but she'll give it all up to do the right thing. When she walks off a film set and flies home to protest what the government is doing to her beloved hometown, she stumbles onto a bigger conspiracy with deadly intentions.

Former Navy Seal Nasir has dealt with his share of high-profile clients, but when he protects a high-value target from a sniper's bullet, he finds himself in the middle of an international terror plot.

Now he feels compelled to keep Chloe safe. The only question is, will the fiercely independent and outspoken actress accept his help?

Charlie, a well-respected researcher, knows everyone has secrets, but when she uncovers secrets at work, that changes everything.

Soon, she finds herself in a terrible predicament of her own making and needs to enlist the help of a handsome former Navy Seal and his security team. But going toe-to-toe with the Mob proves much more dangerous than anyone expected.

Can Nicco and his team keep her out of harm's way or are the Mob's tentacles too long and too well-connected?

ORDER OF SERIES: ANTONIO AND SABRINA DARK MAFIA UNIVERSE

Order of Reading

The Early Years-A Prequel Short Story
https://books2read.com/u/49Zjnw
Antonio and Sabrina Struck In Love Book 1
https://books2read.com/u/4AxKLo
Antonio and Sabrina Struck In Love Book 2
https://books2read.com/u/bpED6g
Antonio and Sabrina Struck In Love Book 3
https://books2read.com/u/3LpgdJ
Janice and Carlo Captivated By His Love
https://books2read.com/u/b6je6M
Antonio and Sabrina Struck In Love Book 4
https://books2read.com/u/4NQyE9
Joaquin Fuertes-The Fuertes Cartel Book 1
https://books2read.com/u/mvZlgV
Joaquin Fuertes-The Fuertes Cartel Book 2
https://books2read.com/u/4DWwLd
Antonio and Sabrina Struck In Love Book 5
https://books2read.com/u/b5kZ8O

Joaquin Fuertes-The Fuertes Cartel Book 3
https://books2read.com/u/4A5LGp
The Carrington Cartel

ORDER OF HEART OF STONE UNIVERSE

Heart of Stone Book 1 Emery and Jackson
https://books2read.com/u/boWPAV
Heart of Stone Book 1.5
https://books2read.com/u/mKELYZ
Heart of Stone Book 2 Jordan and Damon
https://books2read.com/u/ba2OMx
Heart of Stone Book 3.5 Bottoms Up
https://books2read.com/u/4EkjBg
Heart of Stone Book 3 Angela and Brent
https://books2read.com/u/31rx9l
Heart of Stone Book 4 Jessica and Joseph
https://books2read.com/u/4NXyPG

ABOUT THE AUTHOR

Chiquita Dennie is an author of Contemporary, Romantic Suspense, Women's Fiction, and Erotic Romance. She lives in Los Angeles, CA. Originally from TN and before she started writing contemporary romance, she worked in the entertainment industry on notable TV shows including the Dr. Phil show, Tyra Banks show, American Idol, and Deal or No Deal. But her favorite job is the one she's now doing full time – writing romance.

A Best-Selling Author and Award-winning Filmmaker, her first short film, "Invisible," released in Summer 2017 and screened in multiple festivals and won for Best Short Film. She also hosts a podcast that showcases the latest in Beauty, Business, and Community called "Moscato and Tea." Her debut release of Antonio and Sabrina Struck In Love has opened a new avenue of writing that she loves.

If you want to know when the next book will come out, please visit my website at http://www.chiquitadennie.com, where you can sign up to receive an email for my next release.

WHAT'S NEXT?

Want to know what happens next?

Follow me on my website to catch the next release.

Reviews are the lifeblood of the publishing world. They're read, appreciated, and needed.

Please consider taking the time to leave a few words on your review platform of choice.

Sign up for updates and sneak peaks at the site below. www.chiquitadennie.com

ACKNOWLEDGMENTS

I want to dedicate this to my team who helps me behind the scenes, from my editors, test readers, graphic designers, and the list goes on. I truly appreciate each of you for keeping me on my toes.

CATALOG OF RELEASES

By Chiquita Dennie:

Temptation

The Early Years-A Prequel Short Story

Antonio & Sabrina: Struck in Love, Books 1, 2, 3, 4

Janice & Carlo: Captivated by His Love

Heart of Stone, Book 1: Emery & Jackson

Heart of Stone, Book 1.5: Emery & Jackson, A Valentine's Day Short Story

Heart of Stone, Book 2: Jordan & Damon

Heart of Stone, Book 3: Angela & Brent

Heart of Stone, Book 3.5 Jessica &Joseph Bottoms Up

Joaquin Fuertes (The Fuertes Cartel Book 1)

Cocky Catcher (A Hero Club Novel)

Bossy Billionaire (A Hero Club Novel)

Love Shorts-A Collection of Short Stories

Thank you so much for reading and if you enjoyed the crazy ride and decide to leave a review we'd truly appreciate the support.

304 PUBLISHING COMPANY

We showcase authors writing African American, interracial, women's fiction, urban romance, erotic, and contemporary romance novels. Along with thriller, suspense, poetry, beauty, and style books. Thank you for taking the time out to visit. Join our mailing list to stay updated with new releases and blog posts.